THE GREAT BETRAYAL

THE GREAT BETRAYAL:
Arctic Canada Now

by Farley Mowat

with photographs by Shin Sugino

An Atlantic Monthly Press Book

Little, Brown and Company   BOSTON/TORONTO

Canada North
Copyright © 1967 by McClelland and Stewart Limited
The Great Betrayal
Text copyright © 1976 by McClelland and Stewart
Limited, under the title of *Canada North Now*
Photographs copyright © 1976 by Shin Sugino

LIBRARY OF CONGRESS CATALOG CARD NO. 76-40580

FIRST AMERICAN EDITION

ISBN 0-316-58694-3

Maps by James Loates

Portions of the text originally appeared in
Canada North by Farley Mowat.

ATLANTIC-LITTLE. BROWN BOOKS
ARE PUBLISHED BY
LITTLE. BROWN AND COMPANY
IN ASSOCIATION WITH
THE ATLANTIC MONTHLY PRESS

Printed in Canada

Sixteen-page sections of photographs by Shin Sugino
appear after pages 96 and 128. These were especially
commissioned for this book and taken in the Mackenzie
Delta area in the summer of 1976.

Acknowledgements

The information used in this book has come from so many sources that it is not practicable to list them all. I am very grateful to all those who have provided me with information and with assistance of one kind and another, but I wish especially to thank the following organizations and individuals: Inuit Tapirisat (The Eskimo Brotherhood of Canada); the Canadian Arctic Resources Committee, with special reference to Dr. Douglas Pimlott and Mr. Kitson Vincent; Mr. Everett Peterson of Western Ecological Services Ltd.; Dr. Edgar J. Dosman of York University; Mr. Alan Cooke, formerly of the Scott Polar Institute; and Miss Frances Thomson, whose diligence and perseverance have been invaluable.

F.M.

Books by Farley Mowat

People of the Deer
The Regiment
Lost in the Barrens
The Dog Who Wouldn't Be
Grey Seas Under
The Desperate People
Owls in the Family
The Serpent's Coil
The Black Joke
Never Cry Wolf
Westviking
The Curse of the Viking Grave
Canada North
This Rock Within the Sea (with John deVisser)
The Boat Who Wouldn't Float
The Siberians
A Whale for the Killing
Wake of the Great Sealers (with David Blackwood)
The Snow Walker
The Great Betrayal: Arctic Canada Now

Edited by Farley Mowat

Coppermine Journey
Ordeal by Ice
The Polar Passion

Contents

Prologue
The Northern Myths

*Somewhere far to the north of Newfoundland, the St. Law-
rence Seaway, Place Ville Marie, the Macdonald-Cartier
Freeway, the bald-headed prairies and Stanley Park lies an
unreal world conceived in the mind's eye, born out of fantasy
and cauled in myth. Home of the ice worm and the igloo, of
mad trappers and mushing Mounties, of pingos and polar
bears, of the legions of the damned conjured into being by
Robert Service, its voice is the baleful rustle of the aurora
borealis, the eerie howl of Jack London's malemutes and the
whining dirge of Canadian Broadcasting Corporation wind
machines. It is a "white hell," "the ultimate desolation," "a
howling wasteland," "the Land God Gave to Cain."*

*This North, this Arctic of the mind, this frigid concept of a
flat and formless void of ice and snow congealed beneath the
impenetrable blackness of the polar night, is myth! Behind it
lies a real world, obscured in drifts of literary drivel and buried
under an icy weight of obsessive misconceptions; yet the magnificent reality behind the myth has been consistently rejected
by most Canadians since the day of our national birth.*

Canada North, 1967

When I wrote these words, Canada's North was still what it
had always been to the majority of southern Canadians –
terra incognita, a land to be shunned, leaving it free to others
to do with it as they wished. This had been the pattern since
the very beginning of Canadian nationhood.

The exploration of our far northern regions was accomplished in the main by British, French, Scandinavian, German, even Portuguese, adventurers—men who penetrated the myth and took their knowledge of the reality back with them to their native lands. It was their compatriots, not Canadians, who followed up these discoveries. It was English, Scotch, French and American traders (such as the Hudson's Bay Company, Revillon Frères, Canalaska Trading Company, operating out of London, Paris and Seattle) who undertook the first "development" of the North—exploiting its animal and human resources, the while maintaining and elaborating on the northern mythology in order to discourage competition and perhaps also to conceal what they were doing from the myopic view of the people of southern Canada. Even the missionaries, coming in time-honoured fashion in the wake of trade, were aliens. Moravians from Germany and Grenfell from England worked the Labrador. Throughout the rest of the North, Oblate priests from Belgium, Germany and France competed for the souls of the native peoples with Anglican priests straight out from England. The Arctic seas were ruthlessly hunted by Scotch and Yankee whalers. White trappers moving in on the ancestral lands of Indians and Eskimos were almost exclusively northern Europeans. Even Canada's standard bearers of a token sovereignty, the North West (later Royal Canadian) Mounted Police, initially took most of their recruits from England, Scotland and Newfoundland.

Prior to World War II the Canadian North was a part of Canada in little more than name alone. After the War even this nominal possession began to be eroded by a new alien invasion—that of the U.S. military which, during the 1950s, was permitted to achieve something perilously close to de facto control over much of the Canadian Arctic.

As the 1950s ended, most southern Canadians were unperturbed by what had happened and was still happening in the North. Successive federal governments had acted, and continued to act, as if the North was of no moment in the future of the nation. But there were some Canadians, myself among them, who were convinced that in Canada's continuing rejection of the northern regions lay the makings of national disaster. We believed that the *laissez faire* policy of government, coupled with the passive acceptance of the northern myth by southern Canadians as a whole, could result in the loss to Canada of a vast and invaluable territory, even as Alaska had been lost to Russia through very similar causes. We believed that even if Canada *did* retain nominal ownership of the North, our continuing neglect of it would lead to its physical ruination as well as to the ultimate dissolution of the native Northerners: the Indians and Métis of the taiga forests, and the Eskimos of the tundra, the coasts and the Arctic islands.

It seemed to us that disaster could only be averted if southern Canadians could be made to comprehend the true nature of the North, to realize what was happening there behind the mythic camouflage, and so be persuaded to involve themselves in that far country and make it an integral part of Canada. To this end we worked to dispel the prevailing myths of a bitterly hostile and barren land, an essentially worthless land, an uninhabitable land.

The original edition of *Canada North*, issued in 1967, was an attempt at myth-breaking, but it was also designed to entice (or shame – whichever best served the purpose) southern Canadians into taking an effective and informed interest in their neglected northern realm. I tried to paint the majesty and fascination of the North using both words and pictures; I described something of the true history and nature of its native peoples, and I laid perhaps too much stress on the land's potential resources in the hope that these might provide an incentive to encourage Southerners to settle the North in an enduring manner, even as the Canadian prairies were settled not so very long ago. Rightly or wrongly I believed then that an increased number of permanent settlements predicated on carefully planned and cautiously executed development would finally establish Canadian control over what amounts to more than half of our national territory, and at the same time would provide the conditions the native peoples needed to rebuild their shattered lives and so escape from the rigidly colonial rule which had previously doomed them, and the North itself, to despoliation and degradation. Furthermore, I believed that such a venture, entered into on a national scale, might serve to invigorate and unite a nation that was sinking into the divisive squabbles engendered by *la dolce vita*, and so give us a fighting chance to generate some of the greatness of spirit which results when high enterprises are undertaken in a worthy cause.

Now a decade has passed and a new conception of the North has come into being . . . but it is not the one I, and those like me, had in mind. A few of the old myths have indeed been banished, but others have been invented which are of even more fatal consequence. Southern Canadians are now being hoodwinked into seeing the North as a cornucopia of riches in an otherwise useless wilderness, which ought to be immediately drained off southward. They are being traduced into opening the northern doors to admit yet another (and the most deadly) invasion of alien interests – this time the multi-national corporations who owe allegiance to no nation and whose worldwide empires are built on the exploitation of the natural resources of client countries. Southern Canadians are being further deluded into believing that *they* will be the recipients of the lush benefits which will attend upon this act of ravishment; whereas the truth is that Canada's short-term return from the bloodletting of the North's natural wealth has always been, and unless drastic steps are taken will continue to be, measurable in nickels and dimes. The *long*-term reward will be a ruined and devastated land.

No attempt is being made to establish self-sustaining and internally viable settlements of southern Canadians in the North. The only new settlements in view are ones designed to service the rapid removal of the North's resources or to provide bases for a continuing colonial administration to preside over that removal.

As for the native peoples whose land this was, *and is*, they are in grave danger of being so completely overrun by the corporate buccaneers hurrying to help themselves from the North's treasure chest that their future is even more threatened than it was ten years ago.

Southern Canadians and northern Canadians alike are being swindled and robbed. However, the northern natives are at least aware of what is happening and of what the inevitable consequences must be. As a result they are uniting to fight for their own survival and for the survival of their land.

It is my hope that southern Canadians who read this 1970s' version of *Canada North* will gain from it some conception of the true northern reality–past and present; will find in it cause to abandon their lethargic acceptance of a national catastrophe in the making, and will be impelled to emulate the example of the native Northerners and act with them to save our common heritage . . . while there is still time.

I

The Nature of the Beast

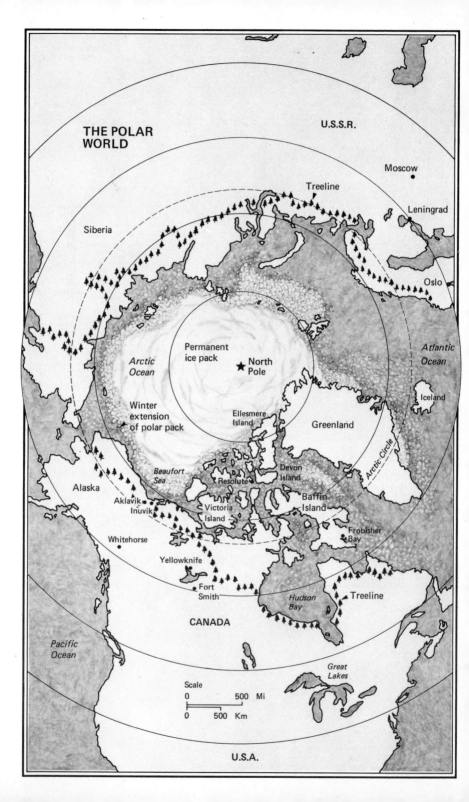

The first difficulty that must be mastered in understanding the northern reality is to decide just where the North begins and to ascertain its boundaries. Ask a scientist for a definition of "north" and you are instantly ears deep in boreal, subarctic and arctic zones, in isotherms, degree-days and permafrost limits. The truth is that the region has no arbitrary southern boundary except insofar as one exists in us as a state of mind. The situation is akin to that of an astronaut shot up in a rocket. At what level does he enter space? At no specific level, but at the moment he becomes aware that he has entered a different world.

For most Southerners the North starts somewhere in the upper reaches of the taiga – the broad band of mainly coniferous forest that sweeps across the entire width of Canada. For others, it has its beginning in the southern marches of the tundra, that immense swath of arctic prairie which lies between the forests and the shores of the polar sea and spreads out over the Arctic islands. However, tundra and taiga are separated by no clearly defined boundary. They meld into one another. Nor does this area of intermix run neatly across the continent due east and west. It begins in the northwest corner of Yukon Territory close to the arctic coast, then slopes off *south*eastward to within a few miles of Churchill on Hudson Bay. Here it plunges almost due south as far as the top of James Bay, then reverses direction and angles *north*eastward across the Quebec-Labrador peninsula finally to reach the Atlantic shore near Nain in Labrador.

One result of the peculiar behaviour of what is sometimes called "treeline" is that, in the far west, it is the taiga which dominates the North, pushing down the valley of the Mackenzie River nearly to the Arctic Ocean; whereas most of the eastern portion of the Far North is dominated by tundra which pushes so deeply south that it brings polar bears and barrenland caribou into the northern tip of Ontario.

Taiga and tundra between them comprise the terrestrial portion of our northern world and occupy an enormous portion of Canada – more than two million square miles, or better than half the nation's total area. Equally impressive is the fact that Canada's Arctic Ocean coastline is longer than her Atlantic and Pacific coastlines put together. The North *fronts* on this third ocean (which is a true mediterranean – surrounded by land – sea) in the same way North Africa fronts on the European Mediterranean Sea. This may seem startling but it is a concept we would be well advised to get used to since Asia, Europe and North America all face each other across the almost land-locked polar sea and it is here that the three continents lie closest together. The impression we get from looking at standard maps that show the North Pole at the top of beyond is arbitrary and wrong. This is not the way the world really is. The polar region is actually the *centre* of the Northern Hemisphere, and the geographical centre of Canada is in the Keewatin tundra two hundred and fifty miles northwest of Churchill. Consequently, when we turn our backs on the North we are turning our backs on Europe and Asia as well as on a great part of our own country. So far only military men, preoccupied as they are with death and destruction, have grasped this vital fact. When and if Canadians find the sense to appreciate its peaceful significance, we may become a nation at the centre instead of remaining a sycophantic satellite at the back door of the United States.

One of the most enduring misconceptions we have about our North is that it is all of a piece – or, at the most, of two pieces: a bleak expanse of frozen sea and a dreary wilderness of frozen forest and tundra. The truth is that the North displays as much variety as any other great natural realm on earth. Stretching northward from the central Labrador coast to Ellesmere Island, the uptilted eastern edge of the Canadian Shield forms a shaggy range of glacier-encrusted mountains that are as massively impressive as any in the Rockies. Although there is nothing to match them in eastern North America, they are unknown to most of us. They form the eastern wall of the North. Far to the westward, beyond the Mackenzie River, rise range after range of mountains that culminate in the St. Elias massif whose glacier-shrouded peaks soar to more than twenty thousand feet. This is the western wall. Between these sprawls the worn and pitted face of the Canadian Shield composed of some of the oldest rocks on earth and so eroded by the work of eons that only the time-smoothed stubs of its once-mighty mountains remain as undulating hills, giving relief to a tundra- and taiga-covered land. Here in the Shield country lies the greatest assemblage of lakes upon our planet. Between the western edge of the Shield and the Yukon Cordillera lies a broad trough of taiga lowlands that extends north from the Great Central Plains of North America. One of the mightiest rivers, the Mackenzie, carries the waters of the Peace, Liard, and many other rivers down this trough to the Arctic Ocean.

North of the mainland lies the Canadian Arctic Archipelago, some hundreds of thousands of square miles of lands constituting the largest island group on earth. These islands, too, have great variety. Some are mountainous; others are low and grassy plains barely rising above the sea's surface. Surrounding them lies a complex of sounds and channels as intricate as the most sophisticated maze. Together the Canadian Arctic islands have a coastline of 26,000 miles – greater than the circumference of Earth.

Also contained within the northern realms of Canada is a vast inland sea, of which Hudson Bay is a part, and into which the British Isles could be sunk without a trace. East of the northern land mass the Labrador Current, carrying a tremendous burden of ice, flows down through Baffin Bay and Davis Strait, stretching an arctic tentacle as far south as Nova Scotia. The polar ocean is itself a species of "land," for it is perpetually ice covered and, though the ice moves, men travel over it and aircraft land upon it.

Although the bone structure of most of the North, the Canadian Shield, is perhaps five million years old, much of the land looks new. This is because a mere ten thousand years ago the entire region, except for the extreme north-western corner, lay buried beneath a gigantic ice sheet. The dome of the Keewatin glacier was at one time two miles thick. Its own titanic weight made the ice plastic and forced it to flow implacably in all directions outward from its high-domed centre. It scoured and gouged the ancient rocks, shearing off the surface soil layers and leaving behind an intricate pattern of water-filled valleys, basins and deep coastal fiords. When the ice eventually melted, it left the land littered with glacial debris and it embossed the naked bones of the country with a complex design of moraine ridges, drumlins and long sinuous eskers of sand and gravel.

Remnants of the ice sheet itself still survive. In the wall of the eastern mountains some sixty thousand square miles of glaciers crown the heights and fill great valleys. Other glacial remnants persist in the mountains of the west.

The bitter climate of that period had another, unseen effect. It deep-froze the rock beneath it, producing perma-frost which, in the extreme northern islands, penetrates fif-teen hundred feet into the primeval rock. Even as far south as northern Manitoba the ancient frost remains only a few feet below the surface layers that thaw in summer.

One of the more abiding myths about the North is that its climate is so hostile that only polar bears and Eskimos can endure it. Yet winter blizzards on the western prairies can match the worst weather the North produces. Northern resi-dents who have subsequently endured a winter in Saskatoon or Winnipeg have even been heard to refer with nostalgia to the North as "the banana belt." Surprisingly, it is a dry world with very little rain or snowfall. Mid-winter snows lie deeper in Ottawa or Montreal than in most parts of the North. Although not even the Yellowknife Chamber of Commerce would dare to call northern winters balmy, they are as bearable as-if longer than-the winters in Toronto, and the summers can be lovely. There are only two true seasons: winter and summer, the transitions between them being so brief as to be negligible. North of the Arctic Circle the midsummer sun never sets and temperatures sometimes persist in the comfortable sixties and higher for days on end. Winter above the Circle sees the sun vanish for weeks or months, but this "long night" is seldom really dark. The northern lights give a pervading luminosity, and the glitter of the stars in a lucid atmosphere, often reinforced by bright moonlight, provides enough light for almost all normal activities.

The concept of the Far North as a barren land is a particularly grotesque illusion. The taiga includes goodly stands of black-and-white spruce, jack pine, larch, birch and poplar; and although the northward-marching trees grow sparser and more stunted until, on the edge of the vast tundra plains, they become the "Land of Little Sticks," the two regions interpenetrate like the clasped fingers of gigantic hands. There are pockets of tundra deep inside the forest, and oases of trees far out on the sweep of the tundra plains. Nor is the tundra itself all of a kind. There is alpine tundra high on mountain slopes, shrub tundra close to the taiga borders, sedge tundra to the north, moss-and-lichen tundra still farther north and, on the extreme northern islands, fell-field tundra where creeping vegetation makes its stubborn attempt to occupy the remote lands that lie surrounded by unyielding polar ice. In summertime most tundra regions boast a great array of flowering plants of infinite number and delight. Although these are mostly small, they mass in such profusion that they suffuse hundreds of square miles with shifting colour. They form a Lilliputian jungle where hunting spiders, bumblebees, small and delicate moths and butterflies abound. Black flies and mosquitoes also abound, alas.

Birds are abundant almost everywhere. Mammals of many species occupy the lands. On the tundra they range from squat, rotund lemmings to shaggy muskoxen; and in the taiga, from minute shrews to massive moose. The seas are home to several kinds of whales, seals, obese walrus and sinuous white bears. The seas are also rich in fishes, as are the numberless inland lakes and rivers. For those with eyes to see, the North is vitally and vividly alive. Long, long ago, men of other races out of another time recognized this truth and learned to call the northern regions "home."

II

The Northern Blood

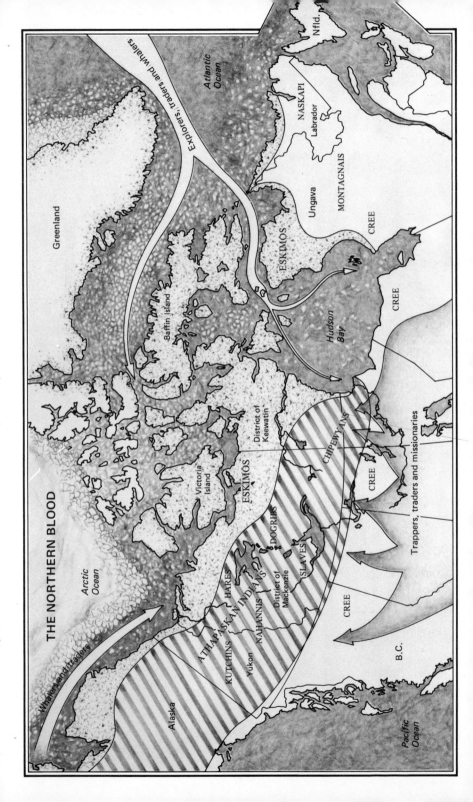

At least seven thousand years ago caribou were dying on the tundra and in the taiga with stone points embedded in their flesh. Quartz flakes, the debris of unknown tool-makers, still lie in profusion along ancient gravel beaches that now cling crazily to hillsides hundreds of feet above present water levels as the central region of the North continues to rise, infinitely slowly, rebounding from the removal of the weight of the great ice sheet. Green hummocks, hollows and circles along river banks and on the sea coast show where now-forgotten peoples once lived and fertilized the ground with the debris thrown out by generations of hunters' wives. On high ridges mute mounds of shattered rock resist the millenniums although the human bones they once concealed have long since vanished.

Men came early to the North. Some evidently came from Asia, entering the North American continent along a narrow corridor of unglaciated tundra lying between the Alaskan Brooks Range and the polar sea. Reaching the mouth of the Mackenzie River these ancient travellers found a human void waiting to be filled. Although the ice sheet had only just retreated and the climate must have been harsh, they moved steadily east, possibly meeting other men who had crossed from Europe by way of the island chain in the North Atlantic Ocean and who were moving west. Some of these unknown peoples were the ancestors of the many-faceted race whose members now collectively call themselves Dene – The People – and whom we know by the generic name of Athapaskan

Indians. When Europeans first reached the northwestern regions in the late eighteenth century, the Athapaskans had long been in occupation of the northern portions of the prairie provinces and British Columbia, together with the whole of the wooded regions of Yukon Territory and the Northwest Territories. They probably numbered close to one hundred thousand.The largest single group, the Chipewyans,controlled the country all the way west from Churchill, on Hudson Bay, to the Slave River. The Slavies held the country around Great Slave Lake, while to the north of them were the Dogribs and, north again, the Yellowknives or Copper Indians. Northward down the valley of the Mackenzie were the Hares, and westward among and beyond the mountains were the Nahanni and the Loucheux or Kutchin Indians.

The Athapaskans were not the only northern Indians. Cree people, belonging to the Algonkian linguistic group, occupied the lands around James Bay and the southwest and southeast shores of Hudson Bay as well as the central taiga forests of the prairie provinces; while the Montagnais and Naskapi occupied the wooded portions of the Quebec-Labrador Peninsula. By dog sled, canoe, on foot and on snowshoe, Indians ranged the entire taiga region. The Chipewyans were particularly fabulous travellers who thought little of walking from the western shores of Hudson Bay to the mouth of the Coppermine River and back via Great Slave Lake–a round trip of at least twenty-five hundred miles! Magnificently attuned to the taiga world, the Indians knew the North as we shall never know it. Yet within fifty years of their first contacts with Europeans they had been so savagely decimated by our diseases, especially smallpox and measles, by liquor and by firearms, that they were close to the vanishing point. In 1976 the *entire* Indian population North of 60 numbered only about twenty-eight thousand. These people did not, and do not, live on reservations although many are treaty people whom the federal government undertook to protect forever. Until recently the majority still lived, as they had always done, in small groups of a few families each, dispersed throughout the taiga which was their sustaining home. Now most of the Dene live in one of a dozen or so beleaguered communities in the Mackenzie Valley, largely severed from the sustenance their land once provided and with no substitute way of life upon which to rely. They share mounting uncertainties with the people who call themselves Métis, but who are known in derogation by many Whites as half-breeds. Numbering several thousands in the North, the Métis are arbitrarily treated by the administration as people who should be proud to think of themselves as white, and who are therefore disqualified from most of the few rights which can be claimed by treaty and non-treaty Indians. In fact the white blood in most Métis has been so diluted by time that they think of themselves as truly a native people and their attitudes and way of life are almost indistinguishable from those of their Indian neighbours. In any event, the final fate of both peoples hangs precariously in the balance, for both are threatened with psychic obliteration if not actual physical destruction by the new march of "progress" into their ancient homelands.

Indians were not the only aboriginal residents of the North. Indeed to most southern Canadians the northern Indians are virtually unknown, having been overshadowed by the image of a neighbouring race – the Eskimo.

What and who is this jolly, chunky fellow in the bulky fur clothing standing four-square to the wild winds of a white world? Is he real – the smiling, simple little chap who seems to spend his time posing for pictures at the mouth of an igloo, carving soapstone figures or stitching up little Ookpiks for the tourist trade? Let Jonasee of Frobisher Bay speak for his own people:

"You made a picture of us in your minds, you Whites. Now you believe the picture. You do not even know our name. You call us Eskimo. That is an Indian word. We are *Inuit* – we are *the* people of this land!"

Indeed an Eskimo is exactly what he calls himself, an

27

Inuk, which is to say, preëminently a man. His race may well be the toughest, most enduring, most adaptable of humankind to be produced by half a million years of human evolution.

Before 2000 B.C. his ancestors had already occupied the northerly coasts of this continent from Alaska to northeast Greenland. Presumably these people originated in Asia although some archaeologists believe there was an admixture of Stone Age people from the west as well. Whatever their origins, they were superbly capable. Their descendants came to occupy the whole of the tundra regions and spread south down the Labrador coast, west along the north shore of the Gulf of St. Lawrence, and down the west coast of Newfoundland as far as Cabot Strait. Some may even have crossed the Strait to settle in present-day Nova Scotia. Most lived by the sea and from the sea, but others lived far inland, deep in the Ungava Peninsula and in the Keewatin and Mackenzie plains. There was no major land area north of the taiga which they could not and did not call home, except for the rock-desert islands at the very top of the Arctic archipelago where nothing more advanced than lichens can survive. Prior to their first major contact with Europeans, there may have been sixty thousand of them in what is now Canada. About nineteen thousand (fifteen thousand of whom lived in the Northwest Territories) survived in 1976.

As was the case with the northern Indians, the Eskimos chose to adapt to nature rather than try to overmaster her. Both races discovered and practised the principle that society is at its best when human beings co-operate instead of competing fiercely. It is true they never learned to build high-rise apartments, could not fly (except in the imagination), could not have invented television, and were content to jog along behind dog teams. But then neither did they invent napalm bombs, make poison gas, or manufacture TNT or nuclear weapons. Nor did they pollute, scarify, exploit and despoil the natural environment in which they lived. In the sense in which we use the word, they were not

28

progressive; nor, if we make literacy the basic standard, were they civilized. They had no written languages but experts consider their spoken languages to be among the most expressive and subtle known.

Indians and Eskimos understood the art of living. Contrary to our disdainful view of them, the northern people did not just "exist." Men, women and children took a tremendous and vital joy from the hour-by-hour activities of their lives. They exercised true genius in inventing and constructing essential equipment without benefit of science or technology. The native northern Canadian had not learned to be aggressive or acquisitive. Content with the world as it was, he was generous, friendly and accommodating–and this was his undoing. Traders and whalers used his talents and his lands to enrich themselves at his expense. Missionaries savaged his natural philosophy in order to substitute their own alien varieties. Europeans in general treated him as a species of subhuman animal and at the same time begot bastard children on his women. The delicate balance between man and nature which Indians and Eskimos had instinctively adopted and long nurtured was systematically eroded.

Considering the ferocious character most southern Canadians ascribe to the North, it seems odd that this was the first part of our continent to be visited by Europeans. The forerunner of these arrived in A.D. 982 when, the old Icelandic sagas tell us, a Norseman named Erik the Red skippered a ship from Greenland across Davis Strait to reach and explore part of the east Baffin Island coast. Erik recognized a good country when he saw it; sea mammals and sea birds abounded, while on the land there were great numbers of caribou and other edible beasts.

The Icelanders who colonized Greenland in the tenth century made the most of Erik's western discovery and for at least two hundred years thereafter regularly visited Baffin Island on summer hunting expeditions. They explored south to Newfoundland where their famous, if short-lived, "Vinland" was located, and north as far as Ellesmere Island; and they also established settlements along the west coast of Ungava Bay.

The Scandinavians who brought the first European blood to the Canadian North were interested in the country for its own sake, but toward the end of the fifteenth century other Europeans began to look northward in hopes of finding a usable Northwest Passage around the top of America which would lead them to the riches of Cathay – the Far East. As early as 1508 Sebastian Cabot sailed to the northwest on behalf of England searching for a strait leading to Asia. In 1576 the buccaneering Martin Frobisher took up the search and his voyage initiated a rush to the northwest. Between 1585 and 1587 John Davis examined much of the coasts of Davis Strait and Baffin Bay. He was followed in 1610 by Henry Hudson and later by a score of others who sailed their crank little vessels into Hudson Bay. Not until two and a half centures after Hudson did hope of finding a practicable passage to the west die down. Meanwhile the first explorers had been followed by a different breed: the fur traders.

English traders arrived in Hudson Bay in 1668 and two years later received their famous charter from Charles II which gave them a monopoly of the trade in, and title to, all lands draining into Hudson Bay and Hudson Strait: a private kingdom that turned out to have an area of 1,422,000 square miles! Not content with this, the H.B.C. (Here Before Christ, as it was called with perfect accuracy) eventually spread across the whole of the Canadian North and into Alaska.

During the early nineteenth century the British renewed their attempts to discover a Northwest Passage, this time through the channels of the Arctic archipelago. The quest reached its peak in 1845 when Sir John Franklin with two ships and 129 men sailed west to conquer the Arctic once and for all. The entire expedition vanished and to this day the full story of what happened is not known. However, the immediate result was to send a wave of rescue expeditions among the islands from the west and from the east, as well as overland along the continental Arctic coast. Consequently, the search for Franklin's lost expedition resulted in European penetration of a large portion of the western and northern regions of the continent.

By 1860 the search for a commercial Northwest Passage had been abandoned. Explorers now turned to a more ephemeral goal – the North Pole itself. What followed was a weird mélange of quixotic courage, gross stupidity, hideous suffering and international chicanery. The Pole may or may not have been reached. What mattered was that this pointless quest led to the discovery of the last important land masses in North America, including many of the Queen Elizabeth Islands (the last of which, Meighen Island, was not discovered until Vilhjalmur Stefansson reached it in 1916).

European exploration of the interior of mainland northern Canada had meanwhile been progressing slowly, although it had got off to a running start when, between 1769 and 1772, a young Hudson's Bay man named Samuel Hearne accompanied a group of Chipewyans right across the tundra from Churchill to the Arctic coast at the mouth of the Coppermine River. After that there was little European activity in the interior until 1789 when the Montreal-based North West Company sent Alexander Mackenzie west and north to trace the river that today bears his name. Trade followed Mackenzie and soon the western taiga filled up with fur traders, but it was more than a century after Hearne's great journey before white men saw the central Keewatin tundra again.

Trading companies, independent traders and trappers were not the only hungry ones to follow the explorers into virgin territory. Close behind them came the missionaries, as avid for souls as the traders were for fur. Whalers exterminated the Greenland whale in Baffin Bay, Hudson Strait and Hudson Bay, then turned their attention to the western arctic seas and virtually exterminated the great mammals there. Then gold discoveries sent tens of thousands of white men pouring north and west to grab what they could get. As the twentieth century began, the majority of the intruders who were roaming through the North were high-grading something – gold, furs, whales or souls. It was a lawless land and there was no attempt to prevent the exploitation of the living resources or of the native peoples. Before 1895 there was, quite literally, no Canadian government presence in what are now the Yukon and Northwest Territories and the Ungava Peninsula.

Canada acquired its North by two massive grants. The first came in 1870 when the Hudson's Bay Company was persuaded by the British government to sell its fiefdom to the Crown, which then transferred it to the new nation. At that date this commercial kingdom consisted of Rupert's Land (all the territories draining into Hudson Bay and Hudson Strait) and the Northwestern Territory, which included all the remaining British territory west of Hudson Bay, except for British Columbia.

Canada's second northern acquisition came in 1880 with the transfer to her of all British rights to the Arctic islands, which meant in effect most of the Arctic archipelago. Thus, by 1881, Canada officially embraced the same limits she does today, except for Newfoundland and Labrador. But the nation seemed more embarrassed than pleased by the acquisition of these vast new territories. It was touch-and-go whether she would even bother to uphold her claims. In 1898 the great Klondike rush triggered a move by the United States to annex that rich country. There were those in Ottawa even that far back who felt that any attempt to withstand the Americans would be bad for business. Fortunately not all southern Canadians were quite that spineless and a small detachment of soldiers and of the North West Mounted Police, which had been sent to the Yukon in 1895, managed to impose Canadian law under the Canadian flag.

In 1909 the American explorer, Robert Peary, laid claim to the North Pole and "all adjacent lands" on behalf of the U.S.A. – a claim which embraced most of the northeastern portion of the Canadian Arctic archipelago. One of his associates, Donald MacMillan, was still maintaining this claim as late as 1924 with tacit support from several U.S. senators. Between 1898 and 1902 a Norwegian, Otto Sverdrup, explored much of Ellesmere Island, most of Axel Heiberg and the Ringnes Islands, and claimed them on behalf of *his* country which, fortunately for Canada, did not press the claim. By the early 1900s American whalers and traders had taken de facto control of the whole western Canadian Arctic coast from the Alaskan border to Victoria Island; of the northwestern reaches of Hudson Bay, and of much of the east Baffin coast as well. To this invasion Canada paid no heed until 1903 when a police post was established at Herschel Island west of the mouth of the Mackenzie River. Also in that year a token Canadian government expedition was sent into the eastern Arctic to belatedly proclaim Canadian sovereignty and to establish a police post on the northwest coast of Hudson Bay.

Although during succeeding years several similar voyages were made to wave the flag, Canada's half-hearted show of ownership remained mainly a gesture until the 1920s when Denmark declared a proprietary interest in Ellesmere Island and the Canadian government was forced to plant a detachment of Royal Canadian Mounted Police there in order to prove "effective occupation."

Until 1875 the entire region north and west of Ontario as far as British Columbia was known as Rupert's Land and the Northwestern Territory, but in that year the federal government constituted the provisional districts of Ungava, Franklin, Mackenzie and Yukon. Then, in 1905, the present provinces of Alberta and Saskatchewan were carved out of the southern portion of the federal territories. Finally, in 1912, Manitoba, Ontario and Quebec had their northern boundaries extended into the territories to their present limits. Thus, by 1913, the Northwest Territories consisted of the unwanted leftovers – the Districts of Mackenzie and Keewatin – which shared the remainder of the northern mainland, and the District of Franklin which encompassed the Arctic islands.

These three districts were governed by the Deputy Minister of the Interior (later Mines and Resources) and a council consisting of representatives of the Roman Catholic and Anglican missions; the Fur Trade Commissioner of the Hudson's Bay Company; and the Commissioner of the Royal Canadian Mounted Police. Under the rule of this family compact the social, cultural and physical dissolution of the Indians and Eskimos, and the general spoliation of the North's animal resources, were allowed to proceed without let or hindrance from the government or the people of Canada.

By 1940 the remaining Indians and Eskimos were riddled with tuberculosis, swept by periodic and often fatal epidemics of diphtheria, influenza and measles, and were chronically hungry and often actually starving. Between 1947 and 1954 more than three hundred Eskimos died of outright starvation in Keewatin District alone. The Canadian Eskimo population had declined to about eight thousand individuals and both they and the northern Indians were in imminent danger of disappearing from the world which had been theirs for countless centuries. As of that time Canada's record in her northern territories was little or no better than that of other nations which were engaged in colonialism elsewhere in the world. Whether she was acting with intent or not, Canada was guilty of practising genocide by neglect in her northern regions.

The advent of World War II was the catalyst for change. The immense northern realm, which Canada had been able to ignore for so long a time because of its remoteness and presumed inaccessibility, suddenly began to become accessible as a result of military activity. This activity included the construction of the Northeast and Northwest Staging Routes which were complexes of air bases used for ferrying war planes to Russia and Britain; the Canol pipeline running from Norman Wells on the Mackenzie River to Alaska to supply oil to U.S. forces there; and the Alaska Highway which brought the first road link to Yukon Territory. Then, after 1945, the Cold War resulted in the virtual occupation of Canada North by the U.S. military. Many new airfields were constructed including a huge Strategic Air Command base at Frobisher Bay. Military weather stations were built on the outer rim of the Arctic islands. Most important of all, during the early 1950s work began on the vast radar surveillance systems known as the Distant Early Warning (DEW) Line and the Mid-Canada Line. These were billion-dollar projects which resulted in the rapid development of northern airlines, of new construction and transportation techniques adapted to arctic conditions, and in an immense if temporary influx of workers from the South. By the late 1950s the doors to Canada North had swung wide open and neither government nor industry was slow to see the opportunities which now lay waiting.

Early in the 1960s, under the aegis of Prime Minister John Diefenbaker's "Northern Vision," the old ruling junta consisting of the missions, the Hudson's Bay Company and the Royal Canadian Mounted Police was replaced by a much more sophisticated form of colonialism. Federal agencies moved north en masse not, as the Diefenbaker government claimed, to bring the North into full partnership with southern Canada, but to facilitate the first large-scale attempt since Klondike days to exploit the North's non-renewable resources.

Those provincial governments which controlled their own portions of the North were not far behind. During the 1960s Premier Smallwood's Newfoundland government displayed its first real interest in the interior of Labrador by hurrying to dispose of that region's major resources – hydroelectric power, minerals and pulpwood – to American, German, British and other foreign interests. Next door, Quebec engaged in a similar sell-out under cover of the popular euphemism of the day, "northern development." The remainder of the high North, consisting of the Yukon and

Northwest Territories, became the fiefdom of the federal Department of Indian Affairs and Northern Development. Although its official mandate charged it with protecting and assisting the northern native peoples while encouraging beneficial development of their lands, the Department's real role was to use every available means to encourage exploitation of northern resources at whatever cost to the native people or to the land itself. In order to foster the illusion that the true interests of the North and its people were being protected, a further deception was propagated, to wit: that the Northerners were free to determine their own destiny and make their own choices in proper democratic manner through their own elected Territorial Councils. The truth was, and remains, that the governments of the Yukon and Northwest Territories are captive creatures of Ottawa. Although both have a number of elected members, real power is firmly held by executive councils the majority of whose members, including the two territorial commissioners themselves, are *appointed* by the Minister of the Department of Indian Affairs and Northern Development. These are colonial governments, pure and simple.

Such was the situation in the North when the 1960s ended. But the 1970s introduced an unanticipated new element – the first truly indigenous political development the North had seen since European domination of it first began. This was a development which was not at all to the liking either of government or of its partners, the consortiums of international business interests which together were then about to undertake the ultimate invasion of the North.

What happened was that the native people finally balked. Faced with the clear prospect of having their culture, their land and themselves inundated, and perhaps destroyed, under a massive wave of resource exploitation over which they had no control, they decided they could no longer tamely submit to the kind of colonial rule which by that time had become anathema in most of the rest of the world. They therefore adopted a course of action which was traditionally foreign to their nature. They began creating their own political arms with which to defend themselves. These soon came to include the Indian Brotherhood of the Northwest Territories, the Métis Association of the Northwest Territories, the Council for Yukon Indians, Inuit Tapirisat (The Eskimo Brotherhood of Canada), and C.O.P.E. - the Committee for Original People's Entitlement.

Among them these closely allied action groups represent most of the forty or so thousand native northern people. Tough minded, well informed and led by young men and women who have learned to recognize modern technological society for what it really is, as opposed to what it pretends to be, they are also learning to use its own methods against it when needs must. These organizations have already become a force to be reckoned with and will be increasingly so in future.

Here is how James Arvaluk, President of Inuit Tapirisat, recently expressed his people's feelings:

"Although Canada doesn't regard itself as a colonial power, most Northerners agree their land is a colony. The colonial rulers live in Ottawa though they maintain an elaborate branch office in Yellowknife [capital of the Northwest Territories].... The North is a forgotten colony in the sense that what is out of sight is out of mind. The southern rulers have been telling us for years, 'Just behave yourselves... be quiet ... don't complain' ... but as long as we follow those instructions the rest of the country is content to forget us. Well, we are not extremists. We are not separatists. We have no history of hostility and confrontation ... but we don't intend to be colonial subjects any longer."

This new determination of the native Northerners to have some say in their own destinies was clearly demonstrated during the federal election of 1972 when the people of the Northwest Territories went to the polls to elect a Member of Parliament to the one seat allotted to them. It was confidently assumed that the white candidate for either the Liberals or Conservatives would win handily since, in the past, most northern natives had docilely supported white candidates whether to represent them in Ottawa or in the elected portion of the Territorial Council. This assumption now proved badly in error. The man who won was Wally Firth, a young Métis from Fort McPherson, representing the New Democratic Party. That his victory was no fluke was proved when he was re-elected in 1974. Wally caused some raised eyebrows in Ottawa by becoming the first freshman Member ever to check into the Ottawa Y.M.C.A. rather than the prestigious Chateau Laurier; and by *renting* a suit when he was presented to the Governor General. But he is now taken very seriously indeed as the first authentic voice to speak in Parliament for the North, and in blunt, no-nonsense terms.

> "My friend Bertha Allen in Inuvik once said, 'We are rich under our feet in the Northwest Territories.' Bertha is right. We are rich in gold, base metals, petroleum, hydro power–all things the world seems to want. We are also rich in animals and fish and unspoiled land–things the world is making very valuable by destroying as rapidly as it can.

> "It is my hope that this great potential can be turned into a life of dignity and security for the northern people–not for twenty years, but forever. We are not headed in that direction now. We are on a path that will turn our potential into quick profits for multi-national corporations. I do not call that 'development.'"

III

The Floating Lands

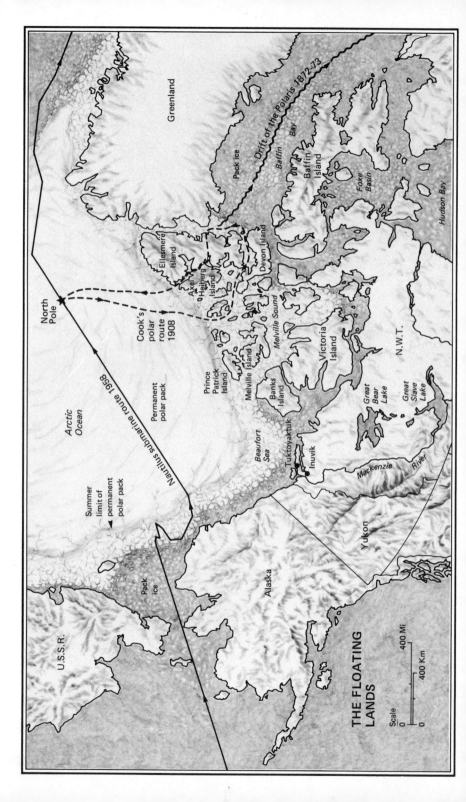

THE FLOATING LANDS

Scale

0   400 Mi

0   400 Km

When geographers of the ancient Greek world conceived of a polar continent lying far to the north of all known lands they were not so far astray, even though what they had in mind was a land of rock and soil. The ice-covered Arctic Ocean, of which Canada claims to control a major portion, is "land" in essence, and one of considerable variety.

Basically this floating continent, surrounded by Asia, Europe, Greenland and North America, consists of heavy ice called polar pack, which ranges from five to fifteen feet in thickness. Driven by wind and current, great sheets of this pack ice crowd against and upon one another to form ranges of hills called pressure ridges. Or they may separate, forming intricate patterns of open water called leads. In some areas there are large salt-water "lakes" called polynias which do not freeze at all. In summer fresh-water ponds and even streams appear on the surface of the pack, for although new sea ice is salty, the salt gradually leaches out, and water melting from old sea ice is quite fresh.

Of real mountains there are none, but they are approximated by icebergs which can be several hundred feet high. These are found in such numbers in north Baffin Bay that early whalers and explorers often mistook them for distant mountain ranges.

As early as 1910 explorers were reporting what they believed to be actual land islands far out in the polar pack. Islands did, and do, exist but they are composed of ice, not rock. They are among the strangest features of the floating lands. Some are only a few miles square but one has been reported which was twenty miles long by fifteen wide and nearly two hundred feet thick. The ice of these islands is extremely ancient – more than three thousand years old, according to carbon 14 tests. Their coasts rise twenty to thirty feet above the surrounding pack and their surfaces are composed of rolling plateaus dotted, in summer, with freshwater ponds and streams. They are probably break-aways from a vast shelf of land-fast ice which projects out into the polar basin from the northern shores of Ellesmere Island and Greenland. Since they were first identified from the air in 1947, more than a dozen of the large ones have been kept under observation and occasionally occupied as scientific or military stations.

In many parts of the high Arctic, land grades into the land-fast ice so imperceptibly that a man can walk off the coast and never know he is over the hidden sea. When flying over the archipelago in winter, it is often impossible to tell whether you are over ice or land. The most northerly islands – Ellesmere, Axel Heiberg, Meighen, the Ringnes group, Borden and Mackenzie King – are almost perpetually welded together by pack ice, so that ice and rock together form one single solid surface larger than Newfoundland.

Parts of the floating land lying close to the coasts are relatively static, but the floating polar continent itself is not. Slowly this whole great world of ice revolves around the polar basin taking as much as five years to make a circuit. The local patterns shift from day to day. While the currents steadily propel the entire mass in one direction, surface winds send portions of it on conflicting courses so that leads open and close and the clash of great pans in collision raises new pressure ridges. Living on the polar pack can be a bit like living in an earthquake zone.

The size of the floating lands is not constant. In "good" ice years the frozen continent shrinks in upon itself and ships can ply far to the north. During "bad" ice years it enlarges until it may block the approaches to the Arctic Ocean as well as sealing off most of the channels among the Arctic islands. Each year the polar pack loses about one-fifth of its area in the form of drift ice that floats south out of the polar basin on two frigid oceanic rivers, the East Greenland and Labrador currents. The pack that comes down through Baffin Bay and along the Labrador coast is often nearly as solid as the polar pack itself–it forms a gigantic ice tongue, studded with icebergs, thrusting down into the Atlantic as far as Nova Scotia. Individual icebergs from it have even drifted as far south as the Azores. But what the floating continent loses in this way it regenerates each winter in the form of newly frozen ice.

Oddly enough, the climate of the floating continent is more moderate than that of the nearby solid lands. At the North Pole the temperature seldom reaches thirty degrees below zero Fahrenheit and during the six months of perpetual daylight–the long Arctic summer–it sometimes rises to fifty degrees above.

Like terrestrial lands the floating ice world has its own life forms. There are no true plants on the surface but there *is* an abundance of animal life. Vilhjalmur Stefansson once spent ninety-six days and walked five hundred miles across the polar pack of the Beaufort Sea, during which time he and his men lived almost exclusively on seals. The Eskimos have always known about the animal riches of the ice world and they spear seals at breathing holes in the pack or shoot them in the leads. Walrus are killed along the fringes of the pack. Narwhals (the sea-unicorn of ancient times) are found in leads far from the nearest open water. Polar bears roam freely over the ice and arctic foxes follow after, scavenging the leavings of the ice king. Dwindling remnants of what were once the largest herds of seals in the world still congregate in spring on the ice driving south to Labrador and Newfoundland where their young are slaughtered in tens of thousands by Canadian and Norwegian sealing interests.

All of these mammals together with many species of arctic sea birds take their livelihood directly or indirectly from the hidden sea below the ice. The polar basin is tremendously deep–some parts of it reaching a depth of nearly three miles. Although the great deeps are relatively sterile, the surface layers can be enormously rich in minute forms of plant and animal life known as plankton. These feed the fishes and also used to feed vast numbers of the great baleen whales that thickly populated Baffin and Hudson bays and the northern coastal waters until they were butchered by whaling fleets in an earlier stage of "northern development."

That man can live and travel on the floating land has long been known. In 1827 an optimistic young British naval officer, William Edward Parry, led a party of seamen on a walk toward the Pole from the island of Spitsbergen, but found that the ice was drifting south under his feet almost as fast as he could trek to the north. It is from the coast of Ellesmere Island that the longest polar walks have been made, culminating in 1908 and 1909 in the possible attainment of the Pole itself by two competing Americans, Frederick Cook and Robert Peary. Of the two, Cook's was the more remarkable journey. Travelling with two Eskimo companions he lived on the floating lands from March 14, 1908, until he regained solid land on July 4, 1909. After them came Stefansson. Born a Canadian of Icelandic parents, he became a naturalized American and, in 1913, a Canadian again. Between 1913 and 1918 Stefansson, by making use of Eskimo techniques, lived and travelled all through the high Arctic archipelago and far out over the ice of the polar sea as well.

These were intentional travels; there have also been some unintentional ones of note. On October 15, 1872, the American arctic exploring ship *Polaris* was nipped in the ice at the very head of Baffin Bay and nineteen of her crew, including (fortunately for the white men) two Eskimo families, were marooned on the pack. They drifted south on it well over two thousand miles until, on April 30 of the following year, they were rescued near the shores of central Labrador by a Newfoundland sealing vessel. During all this time they kept alive and well by eating seals and sea birds killed by the two Eskimo men in the party. There was nothing lifeless or sterile about that portion of the floating lands.

Several attempts have also been made to penetrate the ice continent by ship. Most daring and successful was the voyage of the *Fram* commanded by Fridtjof Nansen. In 1893 Nansen allowed the specially constructed *Fram* to be frozen into the polar pack off the central Siberian coast. The stout little vessel then drifted westbound – a sort of house in the ice – for nearly three years, to emerge from the pack on the north side of Spitsbergen.

The idea worked, but who needed a ship? In 1937 a Soviet party led by Ivan Papanin landed several four-engined aircraft on the ice near the North Pole and set up a scientific station on the floating lands. The Russians remained in residence there for 274 days until they were taken off by a Soviet icebreaker in the Greenland Sea after a comfortable drift of 1,300 miles.

Air exploration of the floating continent began early. In 1897 a young Swede, Salomon Andrée, and two companions set out from Spitsbergen to drift across the Pole in a free balloon. The expedition disappeared; but in 1930 the bodies of the three men were found frozen in an ice bank on White Island east of Spitsbergen.

Since 1914, when the Soviets made the first airplane flight over the polar pack, a steady stream of airborne explorers have flown over the ice continent. In 1926 a flight was undertaken by Roald Amundsen and Lincoln Ellsworth in the dirigible *Norge* and this unwieldy monster successfully flew from Spitsbergen to Alaska. When a sister ship, the *Italia*, commanded by Umberto Nobile, attempted a similar flight in 1928, she crashed onto the polar pack with heavy loss of life.

The Soviets set the pace in Arctic flying. During the late 1930s they sent several aircraft right across the Pole to North America in an effort to establish an intercontinental airline.

45

One landed in Nova Scotia and in 1937 another aircraft flew non-stop over the Pole from the U.S.S.R. to Mexico, then turned back to land in California.

Airplane flights over the polar continent quickly became routine. The Soviets and Americans are now landing multi-engined aircraft on the ice almost at will. The floating continent is even inhabited by man on a semi-permanent basis. Both Americans and Soviets have periodically occupied some of the ice islands and the Soviets maintain many research stations on the main pack.

Not all the polar explorations have been across or above the floating lands. As far back as 1931 Sir Hubert Wilkins conceived the idea of crossing the Arctic Ocean beneath the ice, and the U.S. provided him with an outmoded submarine which he rechristened *Nautilus*. However, it remained for another *Nautilus*, this one nuclear powered, to reach the Pole from the underside in 1958. Since then both Soviet and U.S. submarines have been active in the polar basin, and under-ice voyages have become commonplace.

Surface ships continued to be active too. In 1955 the Royal Canadian Navy's icebreaker *Labrador* made the first northwest passage from Atlantic to Pacific by a deep-draft ship (the passage had been previously navigated only by small wooden vessels).

In 1969 a voyage of quite another kind took place. A huge oil tanker, the M.V. *Manhattan*, owned by Humble Oil (Exxon) and reinforced for ice in collaboration with the U.S. government through funding from the U.S. Navy, was sent *without Canadian permission* into Canadian Arctic waters to test the feasibility of shipping oil from Alaska's Prudhoe Bay through the Northwest Passage to the eastern United States. Moreover, the U.S. government decided to send the United States Coast Guard icebreaker *Northwind* to accompany and assist the *Manhattan*. This decision was also taken without consent having been obtained from Canada. The whole exercise was not only a deliberate challenge to Canadian sovereignty but also, by implication, to Canadian ownership of gas and oil resources which were believed to underlie these waters. Unbelievable as it may seem, the Canadian government not only made no real protest but, when the *Northwind* proved underpowered and unable to assist the *Manhattan*, Canada *volunteered* the services of her own most powerful icebreaker, the C.G.S. *John A. Macdonald*, to help the *Manhattan* and *Northwind* to violate Canadian sovereignty!

The *Manhattan*'s attempts on the passage (she made a second voyage in 1970) were partially successful, but she suffered considerable hull damage which, had she been loaded with oil, would have resulted in a massive spill. Although the true extent of the damage was suppressed, this accident nevertheless highlighted the extreme environmental dangers implicit in any attempt to move loaded tankers through the arctic pack. The threat to Canada's sovereignty was equally apparent and a resultant ripple of public concern influenced the government to enact, belatedly, an Arctic Waters Pollution Act and also to claim a twelve-mile offshore limit (instead of the previous three-mile limit) which would enable her to control the inter-island waterways. Whether she will choose to exercise that control remains uncertain in view of the fact that by 1976 the federal Department of the Environment, under whose jurisdiction the Arctic Waters Pollution Act should come, had *still* not received a mandate to administer or enforce it.

We do not know how successful the *Manhattan*'s voyages were considered to be by the U.S. government and the oil companies which together sponsored the experiment, since neither has seen fit to release any detailed information to the Canadian government, despite several official requests. However, we do know that in 1972 the United States embarked on a crash program to build a number of very large and powerful icebreakers of the polar class. Since smaller and less powerful vessels are adequate in the Bering Strait and for the approaches to Prudhoe Bay from westward, and since the U.S. has no Arctic waters of her own where such

47

powerful ships could be usefully employed, it must be assumed they are intended as escorts for tankers using the Northwest Passage. The assumption is strengthened by the fact that U.S. marine architects, working in conjunction with the U.S. government, are completing plans for sixty-two ice-reinforced supertankers, each capable of carrying 240,000 tons of oil and of making the round trip between Alaska and Cape May, New Jersey, through the Northwest Passage, in twenty-nine days.

Canada is herself contemplating some increase in ice-breaker strength, but it was not until 1974 that the government approved funds for research into polar-class icebreakers and that research will not be completed until 1978. If the government then decides to build one of the new ships, it will not be available for service before 1982. Canada is apparently more concerned to maintain her existing fleet of smaller ships, not for purposes of patrolling and policing her arctic waters but to provide assistance to foreign entrepreneurs wishing to open iron ore and base metal mines in the eastern Arctic.

Unlike Canada and the U.S.A., the Soviets do not view ice navigation simply as an adjunct to resource exploitation. They have long recognized the possibilities of using the arctic mediterranean for general commercial transport. Their nuclear-powered icebreaker, Lenin, has demonstrated that such navigation is possible even deep within the fringes of the ice continent. The Lenin is currently capable of maintaining shipping routes across portions of the Arctic Ocean to North America. The U.S.S.R.'s own Northern Sea Route runs six thousand miles along her Arctic coast from Murmansk in Europe to the Bering Sea. Freighters make the direct run in three weeks and several million tons of mixed cargo go "across the top" each year. The economic potential of the arctic mediterranean as an international trade route remains frozen – not by the climate but by the Cold War. The time may come when the political climate will thaw sufficiently to allow the Arctic Ocean to become a bridge between three continents. If and when this happens, Canada ought to be in a singularly advantageous position – assuming she has not by then lost effective control of her Arctic seas to a more ambitious or more far-sighted nation, and that she has the will to enact and enforce truly meaningful regulations to protect the northern waters and their neighbouring lands.

In the spring of 1976 this possibility seemed particularly doubtful.

Two years earlier Dome Petroleum Limited (an organization closely linked with Gulf Oil and other giants in the industry) had applied for permission to undertake wildcat drilling for oil and gas in the bed of the Beaufort Sea about one hundred miles offshore from the mouth of the Mackenzie River. The Canadian government privately gave approval in principle whereupon Dome quietly began the conversion of two ex-merchant ships of World War II vintage into floating drilling platforms. Government confirmation of the approval in principle would doubtless have been routine even after the news of Dome's intentions finally reached the press. Most southern Canadians who then read about the project were unworried by it, evidently believing – as they were meant to believe – that any action in the North which might provide Canada with more gas and oil was to be applauded. But those who understood the implications of what was afoot were utterly appalled.

The environmental risks involved in attempting offshore drilling within the purlieu of the shifting polar pack are so horrendous that not even the most oil-hungry of the other northern nations has been prepared to accept them. Norway, the U.S.S.R. and the U.S.A. had all previously looked into the possibility and concluded that to permit such a project would be to invite disaster on a mammoth scale. Yet the Trudeau government seems to have had no real doubts as to the wisdom of the decision, even though it must have been fully aware that if Dome experienced an underwater blowout (the term used to describe what happens when a well

49

becomes an uncontrolled "gusher") it would most probably prove to be impossible – due to the shortness of the "open water" season – to drill a relief well and halt the flow *for at least a year.* The Canadian government must have also known full well that, because of the prevailing ice conditions in the Beaufort Sea – which is an integral part of the Arctic Ocean – little or nothing could be done to contain or clean up the *half million or more tons* of oil industry experts themselves admitted could be released by such a prolonged blowout. Hundreds and probably thousands of miles of the Canadian Arctic coasts, as well as the adjacent coasts of Alaska, would be heavily contaminated. Because of the low water and air temperatures, much of the oil from such a spill would remain afloat and adrift for decades and, having entered the arctic gyre – the current system of the Arctic Ocean – some of it would be deposited as far afield as Greenland and Asia while some would be carried into the Atlantic Ocean to threaten the coasts of much more southerly lands. Biologists, considering the probable effects of such a disaster, concluded that the destruction of marine life in the arctic basin would be on such a scale that it could not readily be envisaged. However, Vincent Steen, an Eskimo from Tuktoyaktuk who has spent his adult life hunting sea mammals for a living, had no trouble imagining what the result would be in *his* part of the North:

> "With one big spill the Eskimo people will be finished. There'll be nothing left for us. There'll be no fish to feed the seals and no seals to feed the polar bears, and those polar bears are going to be looking for some white men because they'll have nothing left to eat."

Since the magnitude of the catastrophe which would result from such a blowout could not be gainsaid, Dome and government spokesmen wasted no breath attempting to do so. Instead they blandly insisted that a blowout was next to impossible. They did this knowing full well that neither Dome's two converted ships, nor the special drilling techniques which would be required, would even be pre-tested under conditions approximating those which had to be expected in the Beaufort Sea. They did this by deliberately quoting low blowout figures from ice-free southern fields such as the Gulf of Mexico to show that the odds favouring a major blowout were very small. They did this knowing that the only previous attempt in the Canadian North to drill an offshore well from a floating rig–into the floor of Hudson Bay in the summer of 1969–had been aborted by a storm which drove the drilling vessel off the site, snapping the pipe (which, fortunately, had not penetrated into major oil-bearing strata) and leaving an open hole in the sea bed which the drilling company was unable to cap *until five years later!* They did this knowing it was impossible to predict ice movement in the storm-ridden Beaufort Sea where, at *any time* during the short season of more-or-less open water, the irresistible polar pack could sweep into the drilling area (as it has done several times during recent years) forcing the ships to hurriedly abandon the holes if it did not actually snap the pipes and drills. They did this knowing that if an oil pool *was* found and the drill crew was successful in controlling and capping the well, the bottom gouging effect of winter ice in the region where the drilling was to take place was more than capable of tearing away the cap and so causing a blowout.

In March of 1976, when the Canadian federal cabinet met ostensibly to consider whether the agreement in principle to allow Dome to proceed should be confirmed, the two ships were already on their way northward from their fitting-out yards in California. It was clear that Dome, which had felt secure enough to spend almost $100 million on the conversion of the ships, had no doubt about how the decision would go.

Actually there were several cabinet meetings on the subject and, for a time, it appeared that sanity and wisdom might just possibly prevail, particularly after the U.S. government, which has no great history of standing in the path of the oil companies, asked the Canadian government to delay granting Dome permission to drill, at least until the dangers could be properly assessed and realistic steps could be taken to minimize the risks.

On April 15, 1970, Prime Minister Pierre Trudeau had himself stated the case for caution in terms which can hardly be bettered:

> "The Arctic ice pack has been described as the most significant surface area of the globe, for it controls the temperature of much of the Northern Hemisphere. Its continued existence in unspoiled form is vital to all mankind. The single most imminent threat to the Arctic at this time is the threat of a large oil spill. Oil would spread immediately beneath ice many feet thick; it would congeal and block the breathing holes of the peculiar species of mammals that frequent the region; it would destroy effectively the primary source of food for Eskimos and carnivorous wildlife throughout an area of thousands of square miles; it would foul and destroy the only known nesting area of several species of wild birds. Because of the minute rate of hydrocarbon decomposition in frigid areas, the presence of any such oil must be regarded as permanent. The disastrous consequences which the presence would have on marine plankton, upon the process of oxygenation in the Arctic, and upon other natural and vital processes of the biosphere, are incalculable in their extent."

Exactly six years after he made this statement, Mr. Trudeau's cabinet gave Dome Petroleum Limited permission to proceed with a drilling program in the Beaufort Sea which called for two wells to be drilled each year for four years. Shortly thereafter a Dome spokesman announced that his company was buying and outfitting a third drill ship and would in fact drill fifteen or sixteen wells over a five-year period. The die was cast.

Dome was ordered to post a fifty-million-dollar insurance bond to cover liabilities in case of a blowout or other major spill. This was done in the full knowledge that if such a blowout *did* take place *no* amount of money would begin to repair the damage. It was as cynical a public relations gesture as could be imagined.

Many reasons have been advanced to explain what appears to be an otherwise inexplicable decision. Perhaps the one closest to the truth is that the government was, and is, prepared to take any risk in a desperate attempt to save its grandiose Mackenzie Valley pipeline project. The government is doubtless gambling that Dome will find enough gas and oil to justify undertaking the largest construction project in modern history . . . but one whose value to Canada and Canadians was becoming increasingly dubious during the early months of 1976.

IV

The Icy Mountains

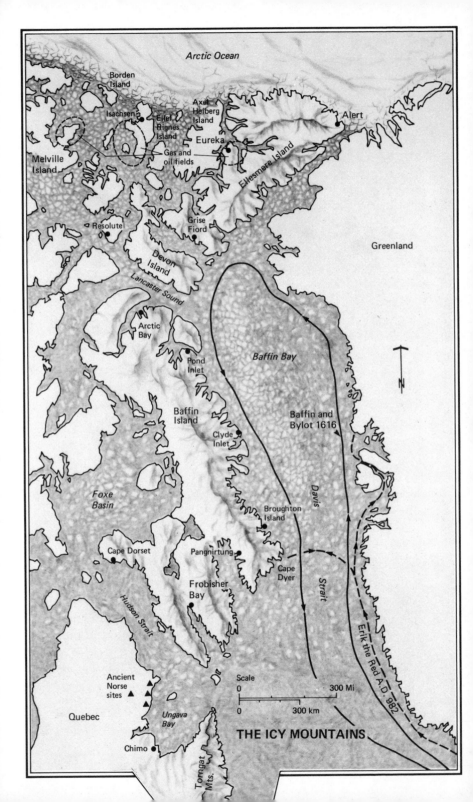

THE ICY MOUNTAINS

Curving up the east coast of Canada like a gigantic sickle runs one of the world's great mountain ranges. Although it is nineteen hundred miles long, few Canadians are aware of its existence. The range as a whole does not even have a name. I have chosen to call it the Icy Mountains.

The southern half, the sickle's handle, includes the mountain peninsula of northern Labrador, ominously named the Torngat Mountains (*torngat* is Eskimo for sorcerer). Standing with their feet in the Atlantic, some of the Torngats' mighty cliffs fall three thousand feet sheer into the thundering ocean. It is a dramatic and desolate region shunned throughout time by men, even by the Eskimos. Almost one thousand years ago Thorfin Karlsefni and Bjarni Herjolfsson, sailing to and from Greenland, were appalled by the grim face of the Torngats. They called it Helluland and described it as a "worthless country." Early Breton fishermen knew it as *terre stérile*, and it is one of the few parts of the North to deserve the name. Despite its comparatively southerly location it is relatively devoid of animal life although the sea nearby is rich in marine life. Much of the interior of the Torngats remains unknown, and most of the white men who have explored its coasts have been inclined to accept the Eskimo belief that it is indeed a haunted land. It is an area which might well be set aside and preserved as a national monument to the world as it was before our coming.

Northwest across Hudson Strait, on Baffin Island, lies the

upper portion of the handle, composed of the Everett Mountains of Meta Incognita Peninsula and the unnamed ranges of Hall Peninsula, separated from each other by the great gash of Frobisher Bay.

The sickle's blade begins at Baffin Island's Cumberland Peninsula in a welter of peaks, fiords and glaciers. Achieving heights of eight thousand feet the blade first curves northwestward across eastern Devon Island, then bends eastward until its peaks occupy almost all of Ellesmere and Axel Heiberg islands, reaching altitudes above ten thousand feet. The tip of the blade seems to be heading for the Pole itself and in fact reaches it – but beneath the surface of the frozen sea. From northern Ellesmere Island the Icy Mountains continue as a submarine range, the Lomonosov Ridge, rising seven thousand feet above the floor of the polar basin (which it divides into two unequal parts), passing over the North Pole and finally emerging as the New Siberian Islands on the Arctic coast of the Soviet Union. If we include this lengthy underwater extension, the whole range is more than three thousand miles long.

The Icy Mountains soar skyward from sea level so that they loom as high above an observer as the famous peaks of the Rockies, whose bases sit some thousands of feet *above* sea level. The fiords gouged into them by the ancient ice sheet are among the most spectacular anywhere and one of them, Admiralty Inlet on north Baffin Island, is the longest in the world. But it is not their size alone that makes the Icy Mountains so impressive: they carry on their shoulders one of the greatest collections of glaciers outside Greenland and Antarctica. These spill down the steep slopes to the heads of cavernous fiords where they calve their icebergs. In the interior valleys moraines left by vanished glaciers themselves loom like miniature mountain ranges of gravel and sand. In addition to the glaciers there are the icecaps, two major ones on Baffin Island, one on Devon, and at least five on Ellesmere and Axel Heiberg islands. These are immense plateaus of solid ice, many hundreds of feet thick, through which protrude the black, broken teeth of buried mountains. The ice-caps alone cover over forty thousand square miles – an area the size of Ireland. They are relics of the ice sheet that once covered much of Canada; now they lurk in the far reaches of the North like insensate monsters, waiting patiently for a colder day when they can begin creeping southward to recover the world they lost ten thousand years ago.

The Icy Mountains seem desolate at first glance, but in some of their deep valleys there is a lush tundra growth and here the muskox is king, attended by wolves and foxes. About the turn of the century the muskox herds in this region were almost exterminated by whalers and by explorers heading for the Pole. They are slowly recovering from the slaughter and there may now be five or six thousand on Axel Heiberg, Ellesmere and Devon islands. Here also is one of the last refuges of the magnificent white wolf, which is elsewhere being harried toward extinction. Arctic hares and ptarmigan are abundant, and the great cliffs harbour colonies of sea birds running into the millions; while hundreds of thousands of eider ducks still nest abundantly on the innumerable offshore islets.

Before the coming of Europeans the sea that roars at the foot of the Icy Mountains was singularly rich, and remnant populations of polar bears, seals, walrus, white whales, narwhals and even a few great whales are still to be found in the south-flowing Labrador Current. At the turn of the century sea and land still provided a good livelihood for some of the most northerly dwelling people the world has ever known: the Eskimos of Smith Sound at the head of Baffin Bay. These people hunted over most of Ellesmere and Axel Heiberg; but now these vast islands, which are together larger than Great Britain, are virtually empty of mankind.

The Icy Mountains were glimpsed early by Europeans. In A.D. 982 Eric the Red probably saw the glittering peaks and ice fields of the Cumberland Peninsula from a mountaintop in Greenland and sailed across Davis Strait to investigate, thereby becoming the discoverer of a new continent. Within a few decades this crossing had become commonplace and by 1250 Norsemen from Greenland seem to have visited most of the coasts of the Icy Mountains.

The first "modern" European to see the mountains north of Hudson Strait was probably John Davis who, on his first arctic voyage, in 1585, reached Cape Dyer on the Cumberland Peninsula. In 1616 Robert Bylot (already a veteran of three incredibly tough northwestern voyages), accompanied by William Baffin, made a complete circumnavigation of Baffin Bay and reached a record northern latitude that held for 236 years. Baffin wrote the subsequent report and so got the credit for one of the great arctic voyages of all time. He and Bylot followed the Icy Mountains south from Ellesmere Island to Cape Dyer, and Baffin plotted the mouths of Smith, Jones and Lancaster sounds. However, these discoveries were so far beyond the sluggish minds at home that Baffin was labelled a liar and for the next two centuries the very existence of the great bay that now bears his name was denied by geographers.

The northern reaches of the Icy Mountains were not seen again by Europeans until 1818 when Sir John Ross repeated Bylot's voyage and demonstrated that Baffin had told nothing but the truth. During the late nineteenth century, explorers by the score sailed north and west through the Icy Mountains searching through Lancaster Sound for the Northwest Passage and later through Smith Sound for the Pole. But the explorers were vastly outnumbered by whalers who hunted Baffin Bay in hundreds of ships. The fiords of the Icy Mountains were used both as whaling grounds and as wintering quarters. Nearly a century of contact between whalers and Eskimos resulted in the emergence of a new, mixed and singularly hardy people on the east shores of Baffin Island. It also resulted in the decimation of whales, walrus, polar bears, muskoxen and caribou.

Farther north, between 1898 and 1902, Otto Sverdrup explored most of western Ellesmere and discovered Axel

Heiberg, Ellef and Amund Ringnes islands and the Findlay islands, all of which he claimed for Norway. Norway hesitated to press her claim long enough for Canada to send A. P. Low north in 1903 in command of the Dominion Government Expedition to Hudson Bay and the Arctic Islands, in the old Newfoundland sealer *Neptune*, to read a proclamation annexing the high Arctic archipelago to the Dominion. Many years later the Canadian government paid Sverdrup's estate $67,000 "in recognition of his work." It was a small price for a land that may, as the result of gas, oil and mineral deposits, be as valuable as Alaska (purchased from Russia in 1867) has become to the U.S.A.

Canada did not attempt even symbolic occupation of the most northerly islands until the mid-1920s when three small Royal Canadian Mounted Police detachments were stationed on Ellesmere and Devon. These stations were soon abandoned except for Grise Fiord on southern Ellesmere, to which a number of Eskimo families had been transplanted to form Canada's most northerly settlement. Two other tiny clusters of humanity exist at the weather stations of Eureka and Alert; but these were established jointly by the U.S.A. and Canada at American insistence and it is a moot question who really owns them.

Devon Island, south of Ellesmere, is now totally uninhabited, but Baffin Island remains relatively populous. Baffin Island looms large in the early history of the exploration of the North, for it was on its southeast coast that Martin Frobisher made his landfall in 1576 during a voyage in search of the Northwest Passage. Frobisher entered the bay that now bears his name (he was convined it was a strait leading to the west), but the discovery of what he took to be gold diverted him to a new purpose. The next year he was back in his "strait" with two ships and the following year he led a flotilla of thirteen vessels to this new King Solomon's mine. The expedition brought with it the first prefabricated house ever to arrive in the North and unwittingly set a fashion that is still much in vogue. When Frobisher's ore-laden flotilla returned home it was discovered that the cargo was only worthless iron pyrite. The bubble burst and the location of the mine and of Frobisher's "strait" itself was lost until 1861 when a Yankee explorer named Charles Francis Hall stumbled upon the relics of Frobisher's base.

If Frobisher could return today he would have trouble recognizing his old stamping ground. The head of his bay is now the site of one of the largest settlements in the Canadian North – and one of the most depressing. During the last war the U.S.A. established a huge military air base at the foot of the bay. A few years after the war the airfield became a major refuelling point for commercial airlines flying piston-engined aircraft on Great Circle routes to Europe. Frobisher Bay became a boom town and the boom was vastly inflated during the 1950s when the Distant Early Warning Line was being built. Hundreds of Eskimos from smaller Baffin Island communities and from other parts of the North were encouraged by the Canadian government to come to Frobisher in order to provide a supply of cheap local labour, to facilitate the policy of assimilation, and because centralization of the dispersed native population eased administrative problems. During the 1960s the apostles of John Diefenbaker's Northern Vision were indulging in prophecies that Frobisher would soon become a great city. Government architects even drew up plans for high-rise apartments to be built under the protection of a gigantic plastic dome. But the advent of jet aircraft which had no need to stop for refuelling soon rendered the great airport all but obsolete. Like all communities based on a single industry, Frobisher Bay was terribly vulnerable. However, there was this difference between Frobisher Bay and a dying southern town: the Eskimo people who were no longer needed locally had nowhere to go. They could not return to the ancestral way of life on the land, partly because they had been suborned into exchanging a hunting-and-trapping way of living for an approximation of "civilized society," and partly because the animal resources they had relied on in times past had continued to decline.

The South did not want them for they were less well adapted to our world than immigrants from Europe. Consequently they became, and now remain, a truly displaced people.

In 1975 the population of Frobisher Bay consisted of about seven hundred Whites, few of whom were permanent residents, and about sixteen hundred resident Eskimos. With few exceptions the only work available was government employment; but the key jobs, as well as most of the minor ones, were held by transient Whites who come north for a year or two on fat contracts, then go back south again for good. One of the first attempts at establishing an independent Eskimo business was started here; but Inuk Limited, as it was called, was unable to survive in the face of White competition. Frobisher Bay Eskimos say, with bitter irony, that it was never *they* who needed the many arms of government (both federal and territorial), it was government who needed *them* – to justify the employment of so many white teachers, administrators, technicians, social workers and sundry others.

By the mid-1970s Frobisher Bay had become a classic welfare settlement. Despite the vast amounts of money spent on it, the town still has no valid reason for existence and no perceived future hope. Canada's first arctic city is a monument to stupidity and bureaucratic futility but, unlike most monuments, its basic material is human clay, not insensate granite. It remains a frightening symbol of the failure of Canada and Canadians to comprehend the reality of the North and to act accordingly. It is a place of limbo, scattered with the wreckage of many broken lives.

The story is not quite so black elsewhere on the Icy Mountain coast. At Broughton Island, Pangnirtung and Clyde Inlet – all on the east shore of Baffin – some Eskimos are still able to make a partial living from the land and sea, but these communities are also in rapid transition. Sealing was always their main source of sustenance but the migratory and once very abundant harp seal upon which they relied heavily is fast being reduced to vestigial numbers by

Norwegian and Canadian commercial sealing on its wintering grounds off Newfoundland and southern Labrador. The children of these small communities go to schools where the doctrine of assimilation into our technical society is the guiding principle. When they emerge from this education system they find it difficult if not impossible to return to the land and the old ways.

The territorial and federal governments claim they have found new ways by which the people can make a living. Heavy emphasis has been laid on craft work, stone carvings, prints and similar products. But the skill and motivation required to make such efforts successful is mostly restricted to the older people who find in these activities some semblance of a functional substitute for the lost life on the land. Very few young people are following, or will follow, in their footsteps. Tourism is another highly touted and equally dubious alternative. There are several new national parks in the North, including Baffin National Park near Pangnirtung which, although it is primarily designed for the recreational use of southern visitors, is supposed to be of economic assistance to the natives. However, neither sport hunting and fishing, nor guiding, produces significant income or employment for the native peoples because the really lucrative elements involved – transportation and lodging – remain in white hands.

"These things they say they do to help us," commented an Eskimo from Pangnirtung. "It is like when a man is starving and you give him a drink of water."

Frobisher Bay is moribund, except as a local transportation and administrative centre, and the communities of the east coast are poised on the edge of dissolution. But the northern tip of Baffin Island shows signs of activity of the sort that appeals to the "think big" imagination of so many southern Canadians. In the 1970s there were still two Eskimo communities at the top of the island, Pond Inlet and Arctic Bay, both surviving, if precariously, on the old hunting-and-trapping economy. However, a few miles inland from nearby Milne Inlet one of the richest iron deposits in the world has been discovered. Millions of tons of ore have been proven, of such a degree of richness that neither concentration nor "beneficiation" is required – the ore can be fed straight into the blast furnaces. Several foreign mining consortiums share interests in this find but are cautious about investing the requisite capital needed to start production. They feel that the short shipping season and the distance to Europe (whither the ore will be shipped) may not allow them a large enough profit. The answer, they suggest, may lie in the use of government-subsidized 250,000-ton bulk-ore freighters assisted by Canadian Coast Guard icebreakers, which would need to make only a few trips each summer in order to remove a year's stockpile of ore. These foreign corporations would also like the Canadian government (that is to say, the taxpayers of Canada) to provide part of the risk capital, as the government has already done in connection with exploration for gas and oil in the Arctic islands.

The full range of mineral resources in the Icy Mountains has hardly been estimated as yet; but along the entire length of Baffin Island one can see exposures of iron ore almost everywhere, and base metal outcrops are nearly as abundant, including a major lead-zinc deposit near Arctic Bay which is now being "developed" under the mellifluous Eskimo name of Nanisivik Mine. The Department of Indian Affairs and Northern Development has hailed this as a great economic opportunity for northern natives and for Canada as a whole. However, the facts are that the mine is almost wholly owned and controlled by foreign companies including a cartel ominously called Mineral Resources International, Metallgellschaft of Germany, and Billiton BV which is a member of the Royal Dutch Shell Group of the Netherlands. Canada does hold a minor equity and will presumably receive something in the way of royalties; but against this the federal government has committed itself to spending 16.7 million dollars to provide roads, a loading wharf, an airport and townsite facilities. This will be in addition to the provision of navigation aids and icebreaker support to the freighters carrying away the ore. Twenty percent of Nanisivik's production of zinc concentrate will go to the U.S. smelters owned by Texasgulf, while the remainder of the zinc and all of the lead ore will go to Germany and the Netherlands for processing. The life of the mine is estimated at fifteen years; and during this time, according to the Department of Indian Affairs and Northern Development, "many Eskimos will be given gainful employment." Very little has been said by anyone of what the results will be from dumping 375,000 tons each year of toxic mine tailings (which will contain zinc, lead, cadmium, copper and arsenic) into nearby Strathcona Sound. But this dumping is almost certain to produce a disaster of the first magnitude amongst the populations of fish and aquatic mammals which have sustained the Arctic Bay Eskimos since time immemorial.

What the exploitation of these mineral resources will mean in terms of human life in the region has not yet been determined, but it is probable that the story of Canada's other far northern mines will be repeated. Some cheap Eskimo labour will be used in the early construction stages, but Eskimos will be employed in ever smaller numbers as the mines become operative. Even assuming that Eskimos wished to work underground, their jobs would last only as long as the ore bodies do and eventually they would be unemployed again. There seems every likelihood that the traditional northern pattern of exploitation of human and natural resources for the benefit of non-residents, and non-Canadians, will be maintained in the country of the Icy Mountains.

V
The Canadian Sea

Greenland

Devon Island

Baffin Bay

Prince of
Wales
Island

Arctic
Bay

Pond
Inlet

Davis Strait

Victoria
Island

Baffin Island

Fury and
Hecla Str.

Pelly
Bay

Igloolik

Iron trough

Pangnirtung

Proposed
polar gas pipelines

Foxe
Basin

District of
Keewatin

Southampton
Island

Cape
Dorset

Frobisher Bay

Baker
Lake

Coral
Harbour

Lake
Harbour

N. W. T.

Rankin
Inlet

Chesterfield
Inlet

Hudson Strait

Chubb
crater

Eskimo
Point

Hudson Bay

Payne
Bay

Ungava
Bay

Povungnituk

Churchill

Henry
Hudson
1610

Port Harrison

Chimo

Treeline

Western

Belcher
Islands

Ungava
Peninsula

proposal

Eastern proposal

Great Whale River

MANITOBA

THE CANADIAN SEA

James
Bay

QUEBEC

Scale
0   300 Mi

0   300 Km

Moosonee

ONTARIO

Although most of us are aware that Canada is bounded on the north, east and west by three oceans, few Canadians realize there is a mighty sea right in the middle of our country. Part of the difficulty is that, like the Icy Mountains, it has no all-inclusive name. We call the largest part of it Hudson Bay (although it is not correctly a bay at all); but this is by no means the whole of it. Canada's inland sea (the name "Canadian Sea" is again my own) consists of Hudson Bay, James Bay, Foxe Basin, Hudson Strait and Ungava Bay, and it is one of the world's three greatest inland seas – the others being the Arctic Ocean, as already described, and the Mediterranean, which is only one-third larger than the Canadian Sea.

The Canadian Sea stretches thirteen hundred miles from north to south and is nearly six hundred miles across at its widest point. Nobody can be certain how such a gigantic body of salt water became trapped in the interior of the continent. One explanation is that the Canadian Sea marks the centre of a monstrous icecap from the Pleistocene glaciation – an icecap comparable to the one which still exists in Greenland and which, like it, grew so weighty that it depressed the earth's crust to form a titanic bowl the centre of which filled with salt water after the melting of the ice. Whatever its origin the bowl now forms a drainage basin of almost a million and a half square miles and is fed by the waters of scores of great rivers including the Nelson, Saskatchewan, Thelon, Churchill, Fort George and Moose.

Consistent with the icecap theory is the fact that the floor of this basin is rebounding at what, in terms of geological time, is a startling rate. The Canadian Sea has shrunk by something like half its area during the past ten thousand years, and its coastal plains for as much as two hundred miles inland clearly show that they were formerly sea bottom. Seen from the air the west coast of Southampton Island appears to have just emerged from the sea with hundreds of old sand and gravel beaches overlapping each other for many miles into the interior. Camp sites of the Dorset Eskimoan culture, which were situated on water-lapped beaches three thousand years ago, now sit high and dry forty or fifty feet above sea level and as much as five miles inland.

The Canadian Sea has other peculiarities. Perhaps the oddest is a great semi-circular bite out of the southeast coast of Hudson Bay. Curving south from Portland Promontory to Cape Jones, the coast forms a remarkably precise geometric arc, part of a circle which if projected to completion would have a diameter of about three hundred miles. The missing part of the circle lies under the waters of Hudson Bay, but roughly in its centre there is a complex of stringy, curved islands known as the Belchers. These display a pattern similar to what glacial and water erosion might do to one of the great upthrust cones within a lunar crater. The Belcher Islands are rich in iron ore that has a composition similar to that of some iron meteorites. A few miles offshore from the mainland arc, and precisely paralleling it, is an almost continuous row of linear islands – the Nastapokas. These resemble what the outer ridge of a lunar crater might look like if exposed to terrestrial erosion. The presence of the nearby Chubb crater in Ungava – one of the largest recognized meteor craters in the world – strengthens my suspicion that southern Hudson Bay may have been the focus of one of the most stupendous meteor strikes in the history of our planet.

The Canadian Sea is entered from the Atlantic through a rock-toothed gap between the Torngat Mountains of north Labrador and the mountains of southern Baffin Island. The mouth is followed by the long throat of Hudson Strait. Just inside this throat Ungava Bay sags south like a huge goitre. The passage opens westward between Cape Dorset on Baffin Island and Cape Wolstenholme on Ungava Peninsula, into the Canadian Sea proper. To the south lies Hudson Bay. To the north lies the relatively shallow expanse of Foxe Basin, bordered by the saturated lowland plains of west Baffin Island and east Melville Peninsula. Foxe Basin is partly separated from Hudson Bay by the triangular mass of Southampton Island and by the lesser barriers of Coats and Mansel islands. James Bay forms an appendix at the south end of Hudson Bay and both it and Hudson Bay are bordered on the west by lowlands that approach the condition of flooded bogs.

In the extreme northwest corner of Foxe Basin a narrow channel – Fury and Hecla Strait – provides a back door out of the Canadian Sea to the westward. Up to now this channel has proved useless for navigation because it is usually choked with ice. However, modern icebreakers would have little difficulty keeping it open if we so desired, thereby providing a passage from the Canadian Sea to the waters of the western Arctic. Just south and west of Southampton, Chesterfield Inlet and Baker Lake together form a sea-route extending two hundred miles west-northwest into the heart of the great Keewatin tundra, with water deep enough for ocean-going ships of considerable tonnage.

The Canadian Sea provides direct access to the Atlantic Ocean from the very centre of Canada. Incredible as it may seem, the sea distance from Churchill, on the west side of Hudson Bay, to Liverpool in England is about the same as the sea distance from Montreal to Liverpool! It is in the north that Canada lies closest to the other continents of the Northern Hemisphere.

This basic fact of geography was very much a reality to early European explorers and in part explains why the Canadian Sea once played a most important role in the exploration and occupation of this country. The first Europeans to reach it – so far as we know – were the Norse working their way down the Baffin coast from Cape Dyer during the decades after Erik the Red discovered Baffin Island. The Norse were great seamen and, like those who followed them, well able to understand the significance of the massive tidal stream which flows into and out of the gaping mouth of Hudson Strait. They called the place *Ginungagap* – meaning a strait leading to another sea. They were looking for good hunting lands and they found these in Ungava Bay, which became known to them as Skuggifiord. By as early as 1100 they had begun to colonize the west coast of the Ungava Peninsula.

How do we know this? Partly because the Icelanders retained a body of sagas that preserve fragments of the Skuggifiord story, but mainly due to the work of archaeologist Thomas Lee who has excavated several large-scale ruins in the vicinity of Payne Bay. One of these is the remains of a stone-and-turf walled structure some eighty-five feet long and more than thirty feet wide with slightly curved outer walls and traces of at least three internal partitions. It is identifiable in all salient features with the typical Norse *skala* or long hall of the twelfth century and earlier. Another of Lee's discoveries is an inland village site where there is a row of square stone ruins neatly floored with stone paving. At one end of this village "street" stands a structure having such a close similarity to twelfth-century Greenlandic churches that its origin can hardly be in doubt.

The question of what eventually happened to the Norse settlers in Ungava may already have been answered. From the evidence of the preliminary excavations it would appear that an isolated Norse culture in the region gradually lost its distinctive features as it merged with a local Eskimo culture. The latest ruins in the series, together with skeletal material, seem to demonstrate the existence of a people who were not quite Eskimo but who were no longer European.

Ungava Bay may be a backwater now, but running north from near the height of land in Quebec-Labrador is a belt of iron formations which extends to and up the west coast of Ungava Bay and continues on up the spine of Baffin Island. This ore "trough" may well hold the greatest single occurrence of iron ore on the surface of the globe. It is already being mined at Schefferville in northern Quebec and at Wabush and Labrador City in western Labrador . . . by multi-national corporations controlled outside Canada. Additional holdings of Cyrus Eaton of the U.S.A. and of Krupp of Germany in the Fort Chimo and Leaf River regions of Ungava are due to be exploited in the near future. International Iron Ore Limited, owned by Iranian and German interests, is currently planning a huge mine at Aupaluk Bay which will require the construction of a town capable of housing five thousand miners, their dependents and ancillary employees. As is the case with all the producing iron mines in Quebec and Labrador, most of the ore will be shipped to foreign countries for processing and subsequent manufacture. This pattern will also hold true for the exploitation of lead, zinc and silver deposits which are to be mined in the extreme northern portion of Ungava.

Ungava Bay has another and perhaps even more valuable resource – its huge tides. At Leaf Bay on the western shore these tides rise as high as sixty-four feet above low water mark – as high as any in the world – and they could be harnessed at Leaf Basin and several other sites to provide virtually limitless quantities of electricity. However, the Quebec government of Premier Robert Bourassa has instead chosen to undertake the multi-billion-dollar Baie James "development" which is designed to produce millions of kilowatts of electricity by damming several major rivers which flow into James and Hudson bays, and by reversing the flow in others, thereby flooding tens of thousands of square miles of the ancestral hunting and trapping grounds of the James Bay Cree Indians. This is the single most devastatingly destructive and iniquitous enterprise yet undertaken in the North and is a prime example of what is really meant by governments and industry when they prate glibly of "northern development."

It can provide little consolation to know that the Baie James project is neither Québecois nor Canadian except in name, since it was initiated at the behest of, and is being largely funded and built by, U.S. interests. Only a fraction of its electrical power is destined for Canadian use. Most of its potential output is already under contract to U.S. utility companies, chief amongst which is Consolidated Edison. Although it will have cost Canada an incalculable amount in ruined and dislocated human lives, and will have inflicted irremediable damage on a vast region of our North, it will do little or nothing to ease the growing energy shortage which faces all Canadians. Baie James represents a sell-out of Canada on a truly titanic scale.

To make the whole affair even more inexcusable, engineering studies, together with pilot projects already completed in other countries, clearly demonstrate that the tidal power available in Leaf Basin *alone* could produce as much electricity, with almost no adverse environmental or human effects, and at much lower capital cost. Then why Baie James? The choice appears to have been dictated by political and financial expediency since the Baie James project will provide more short-term employment for Quebec labour and larger profits to the construction companies involved, not to mention bigger interest payments to the U.S. financial groups who are funding it.

The early Norse explorations of the Canadian Sea were never entirely forgotten. Around 1476 a Scandinavian named Johan Scolvus seems to have piloted a Danish expedition into Hudson Bay; and in 1508 Sebastian Cabot reached, and may have entered, Hudson Strait. The irrepressible Martin Frobisher sailed into the Strait by accident in 1578 when he was trying to get back to the bay now named after him. Then, in 1610-11, the man whose name the Strait and Bay now bear sailed west, poked about in Ungava Bay, cleared Hudson Strait, and sailed almost to the bottom of Hudson Bay where he wintered before being cast adrift by a mutinous crew.

With the Canadian Sea officially discovered by the English, a rush began. Thomas Button, Robert Bylot, "Northwest" Foxe, Thomas James and others hastened to the new sea all hoping to find a passage out of it to the northwest. There was one stranger in their midst. In 1619 the King of Denmark sent out an expedition led by Jens Munk, not merely to discover the Northwest Passage but to reclaim by settlement the lands the Scandinavians had discovered so long ago and upon which the English were now trespassing. Munk's story is a grisly one. He and his men lacked the old Norsemen's ability to become a part of the northern world and, by the spring of 1620, sixty-two men had died of scurvy leaving only Munk and two other survivors, all deathly sick, to make their way back to Denmark in a leaking tub of a ship.

After the Munk disaster the Danes withdrew from the game, but the inland ocean continued to draw Europeans to it. Two French fur traders, des Groseilliers and Radisson, seem to have been the first to grasp the real importance of the Canadian Sea, realizing that it provided by far the most direct ocean route between Europe and the centre of North America. Failing to convince their own people of its worth, they persuaded English merchants to outfit a fur-trading expedition which sailed to Hudson Bay in 1668. The voyage was so great a success that in 1670 a royal charter was granted to the Governor and Company of Adventurers of England Trading into Hudson's Bay. This is a date to remember. From that time forward the inland ocean became (though not without sundry fights with the French and, later, with Montreal-based free traders) the private lake of the Hudson's Bay Company and the entrepôt from which that company spread its commercial tentacles all through the North American west and north.

When the English first reached the shores of the Canadian Sea its coasts were well populated. From Churchill south around James Bay and north to Fort George, Cree Indians lived and hunted. In the vicinity of Churchill the great Chipewyan nation reached the inland sea. North of the Chipewyans a quarter million square miles of the Keewatin tundra was occupied by several thousand Caribou – or Inland – Eskimos. Other Eskimo groups occupied the tundra coasts of Hudson Bay, the interior of the Ungava Peninsula, both sides of Ungava Bay and the coast of Labrador. Around Foxe Basin the seal- and walrus-hunting Central Eskimos lived in large numbers.

In 1912 the federal government ceded the whole of the Ungava territory to Quebec – something it has since deeply regretted. Quebec ignored this vast territory until recently when it too began to have colonial aspirations. Ungava was renamed *Nouveau-Québec* and exploitation of its resources began with the same consequences to the surviving native peoples – six thousand Crees, four thousand Eskimos and four hundred Naskapi – that their relatives in the Territories were already experiencing. A young Cree from Fort George who spent three unhappy years in Montreal had this to say about current developments:

> "It's a pretty funny thing. The way the French say they always been given a hard time by the English. A minority, always put down by the English. Now they do the same thing to us and that's okay for them to do."

Along the east coast of Hudson Bay are three sizable Eskimo communities – Great Whale River, Port Harrison and Povungnituk – and on James Bay are a number of Cree settlements. All were functioning fairly well until recently on a hunting and trapping economy, but the effect of Quebec's new northern thrust, and of the Baie James project in particular, has been to shatter this way of life so that now many of the native settlements are turning into shabby adjuncts to construction camps filled with transient Whites who are rapidly bringing about the collapse of a viable way of life to which the native peoples had stubbornly adhered.

In the 1960s, Povungnituk was a particularly healthy community due partly to the efforts of Father André Steinmann, who laboured not just to save souls but to assist the Eskimos of the region to cope with the outer world. He helped found the Povungnituk Inuit Co-operative which, in 1967, earned nearly $200,000. But now, in the 1970s, Father Steinmann's efforts are being rapidly eroded by the impact of the Baie James development. The changes are calculatedly cultural, as well as economic. Quebec is determined that its culture will dominate in its new colony. French has consequently become obligatory in the native schools where, previously, the primary language had been English. Even the names of the communities have been arbitrarily changed: thus Great Whale River has become *Poste-de-la-Baleine* while Port Harrison now glories in *Notre Dame d'Inoucjuak.*

The most drastic changes, however, are those which affect the native peoples' claims to the land and to a way of life which they have always followed and still prefer. During the mid-1970s the Quebec government "negotiated" land rights settlements with the Eskimos and Indians of northern Quebec. These negotiations were begun *only* after the native peoples, assisted by some few friends in the South, took legal action to resist the arbitrary seizure of their lands. It was a David and Goliath battle, for the Quebec government was wholeheartedly supported by the federal government which, with its own plans for the North, was most anxious to contain the legitimate demands of the Quebec native peoples for fear that an expensive precedent might result. The negotiations were carried out under extreme duress as far as the Eskimos and Indians were concerned because the Baie James project was well under way and it had become a choice of taking what Quebec offered or getting nothing at all.

Although Quebec publicized its offer as being an innovative and generous settlement of native claims, the agreement which was eventually signed was not essentially different from the repressive treaties imposed on most Canadian Indians by the federal government in years gone by. The agreement with the Northern Quebec Inuit Association is typical. It covers an area of 250,000 square miles of what had been Eskimo territory since time immemorial. The agreement "gives" the Eskimo *one* per cent of their own territory in small blocks around their existing settlements – thus in effect establishing a reservation system of the bad old kind. The people were also granted exclusive hunting, fishing and trapping rights on an additional *nine* per cent, but with no ownership or control over it. The remaining *ninety* per cent of traditional Eskimo lands was reserved by the province for resource "development." To sweeten what was a very bitter pill, the Eskimos were also offered cash compensation, which may eventually amount to about $15,000 for each person. All this in exchange for the total "extinguishment" of their hereditary rights to their ancestral lands.

Although the leaders of the Inuit Association felt compelled to sign the agreement, the people of Povungnituk, Ivujivik and Sugluk resolutely refused to do so. As a result they have been "given" no land and will probably receive no compensation. What was theirs will simply be taken from them. The Quebec government calls this procedure "negotiation." Others might well find a different word with which to describe it.

The kind of future development Quebec has in mind for the new colony is typified by an asbestos mine which opened in 1972 at Deception Bay on the north tip of Ungava. This mine, which employs a grand total of two Eskimos, now ships about 300,000 tons of asbestos annually via Hudson Strait to West Germany. The returns to Quebec or to Canada are small enough, but to the people of Ungava they are effectively nil. It is clear that the Quebec government does not feel that the native peoples have any right to benefit from the exploitation of the resources of Ungava. Consider this 1975 statement by New Quebec Administrator, Clement Tremblay:

> "The only potential in New Quebec for the Eskimos is tourism. The Eskimos will never become miners; they will never be the exploiters of their own resources .... They must do what they enjoy and are good at, and that seems to be handicrafts and guiding."

One bright spot does exist on the shores of the Canadian Sea. At Cape Dorset on southwest Baffin Island, a one-time southern Canadian named Terry Ryan is manager of the West Baffin Island Co-operative. A salaried employee of the Eskimos, who are the owners of the Co-op, he has made Cape Dorset his permanent home, and with his assistance Cape Dorset has become world famous as a source of Eskimo art. Ryan is personally famous in the North for having persuaded the Department of Transport to buy several *inukshuk* (piles of stones that Eskimos had erected, partly for fun, on hilltops) for the handsome price of $2,500 each. These are now proudly displayed at Toronto's International Airport.

Elsewhere around the shores of the Canadian Sea the picture is far from bright. Rankin Inlet, on the west shore of Hudson Bay, stands as another monument to the classic results of northern exploitation. A nickel mine which opened there in 1957 was originally hailed as the ideal model for the involvement of northern natives in the development of the resources of their lands. The mine management did in fact hire many Eskimos and taught some of them technical skills. For a short time Rankin became a boom town. Then, in 1962, the high-grade ore began to thin out and the mine was abruptly closed. Today there is almost no employment for the hundreds of Eskimos who were encouraged to move to Rankin Inlet, and the settlement has become just one more administrative centre for the territorial and federal governments with most of its native residents existing on welfare of one form or another.

South of Rankin, at Eskimo Point, things are even worse. In 1976 Eskimo Point had a population of 650 people – 620 of them Eskimos. Some of these are refugees from the Keewatin interior from which they were driven during the 1950s by the mass destruction of the caribou. There is not nearly enough game available near Eskimo Point to support such a large group of hunting people and there is virtually no wage employment. Consequently most of them have no alternative but to live, from one generation to the next, on the dole (supplemented by what little they can make from handicrafts), and in conditions of poverty which make many southern slums appear almost idyllic by comparison.

Eskimo Point is by no means unique. Around the shores of the Canadian Sea live well over ten thousand survivors of the original population of Indians and Eskimos, the majority of them dispossessed of their ancient way of life and with no viable alternative to which they can turn.

The Canadian Sea is surrounded by many running sores. Churchill, in northern Manitoba, is a prime example. It has been continuously inhabited by Europeans for more than two and a half centuries; but it was not until 1929, after prolonged agitation by western Canadians, that a railway was finally completed from The Pas to Churchill, where a large grain elevator and a marine terminal were constructed. It was intended that western grain should be shipped to Europe by the short northern route. Some grain was – and is – shipped by this route but it is a mere trickle – a gesture. Yet with only minor additions to its handling facilities, Churchill could ship twenty times its present volume of grain, as well as other products, and could receive an equivalent amount of incoming freight from Europe for distribution to western Canada. Modern navigation aids, aerial ice patrols, and the icebreakers of the Canadian Coast Guard could keep this northern sea route open nearly twice as long each year as is done at present. But little if anything is being undertaken to realize Churchill's potential as a deep-water seaport ... primarily because of opposition from southern interests which include a major Canadian railroad, Quebec and Ontario ports, and the U.S. and Canadian supporters of the St. Lawrence Seaway. Despite a recent federal-provincial gift to Churchill of a ten-million-dollar community centre which the town does not have enough income to run or to maintain, Churchill remains essentially what it has long been–a decrepit and lacklustre village surviving on memories of better days and tattered future hopes.

Agitation to make more and better use of the Canadian Sea as a shipping route continues, but with small results. In March of 1976 a commission appointed by the Ontario government to assess the worth of a seaport on James Bay reported that, while the idea was feasible, it would be economically impracticable. Yet, as an alternative, the commission recommended building a nine-hundred-mile railroad from the present railhead at Moosonee west and then north along the shores of James and Hudson bays, past Churchill, to distant Boothia Peninsula ... *not* in order to provide Ontario's industrial South with a direct shipping route to Europe via the Canadian Sea, but *solely* to allow Ontario to tap deposits of coal, oil and minerals in northern Keewatin Territory and the Arctic islands. Ontario, with no far-northern colony of its own, does not want to be left out of the northern "development" action.

Although the dream of using the Canadian Sea as a trade route linking the central regions of the nation to Europe and the outer world remains not much more than a dream, changes are in the wind for Hudson Bay. Large quantities of oil and gas are believed to underlie its bed. The first exploratory drilling was done during the summer of 1969 by a consortium-sponsored company, with French affiliations, called Aquitaine. The attempt ended in near disaster when, as noted in Part III–The Floating Lands, Aquitaine's floating rig was driven off the drill site by a storm that inflicted half a million dollars' damage to the rig and nearly sank it. It was only by incredibly good luck that the drill had not reached major oil-bearing strata (although it had passed through traces of both oil and gas) because it was not until 1974, five years later, that the company was able to cap the uncompleted well. Drilling in south-central Hudson Bay is continuing, and two wildcat wells had been completed by the autumn of 1975. Results remain obscure but success is not likely to bring any great or enduring benefits to the communities on the shores of Hudson and James bays. On the contrary, a blowout, or a major accident to a producing undersea well or to the pipelines carrying the oil or gas ashore, would deal a staggering blow to this central region of the Canadian North which is already suffering from the damages consequent upon two centuries of feckless exploitation. Because of the frigid water temperatures and the almost land-locked nature of the Canadian Sea, a major spill would persist for generations and could be expected to destroy most higher forms of marine life such as seals, polar bears, white whales and walrus, together with enormous numbers of migratory waterfowl, including the snow and Canada geese which gather each autumn and spring by the hundreds of thousands on the mudflats of James Bay.

VI
The Northern Prairie

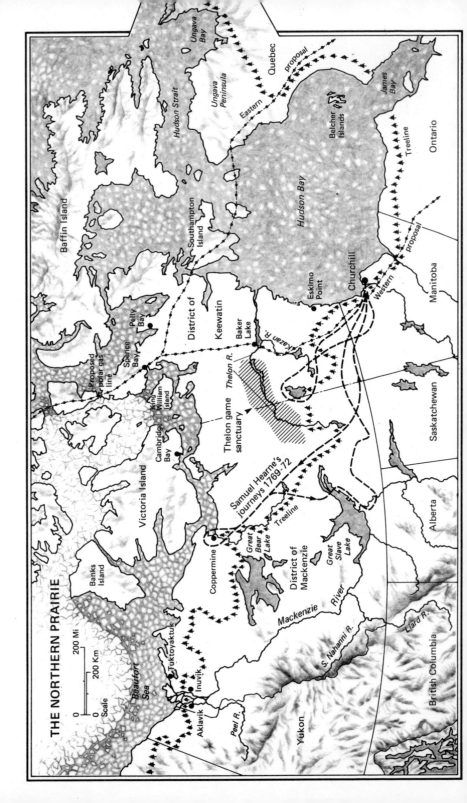

THE NORTHERN PRAIRIE

Scale

0   200 Mi
0   200 Km

Beaufort Sea

Banks Island

Victoria Island

King William Island

Pelly Bay

Spence Bay

Cambridge Bay

Proposed polar gas line

Baffin Island

Southampton Island

District of Keewatin

Baker Lake

Thelon R.

Thelon game sanctuary

Kazan R.

Eskimo Point

Churchill

Manitoba

Saskatchewan

Western proposal

Treeline

Hudson Bay

Belcher Islands

James Bay

Ontario

Hudson Strait

Ungava Bay

Ungava Peninsula

Quebec

Eastern proposal

Tuktoyaktuk

Inuvik

Aklavik

Peel R.

Yukon

Coppermine

Great Bear Lake

Treeline

Samuel Hearne's journeys 1769-72

District of Mackenzie

Great Slave Lake

Mackenzie River

S. Nahanni R.

Liard R.

Alberta

British Columbia

Sprawled across the upper mainland of northern Canada lies a tremendous tract of tundra which for centuries has been known to non-natives as the Barren Grounds, the Barren Lands or simply the Barrens. To the eastward the tundra plains occupy most of the Ungava Peninsula. To the west they form an enormous triangle whose apex touches the Alaska-Canada border at the Beaufort Sea. The northern side of the triangle extends eastward fourteen hundred miles along the mainland Arctic coast to the shores of the Canadian Sea. The southern side runs fourteen hundred miles in a southeasterly direction past Great Bear Lake and past the east end of Great Slave Lake to the shores of Hudson Bay in northern Manitoba. The base of the triangle is the west coast of the Canadian Sea, from Churchill six hundred miles north to Repulse Bay. This western tundra wedge is linked to the Ungava Peninsula by a narrow coastal strip that runs south and east from Churchill to the top of James Bay then north up the east coast of Hudson Bay to Richmond Gulf.

The total tundra of mainland Canada amounts to more than half a million square miles of rolling, lake-dotted plains, broken here and there by ranges of old, worn-down hills. To an observer in a small aircraft droning for endless hours over its seemingly illimitable space, the tundra seems to be as much a world of water as of land. Its lakes, ponds, bogs and rivers are beyond counting. Seen from the air the land appears to be dun-coloured, monochromatic, apparently featureless, reaching to the horizon on all sides with an illusion of interminable monotony.

But this is only an illusion. Look closer and the void of land and water becomes an intricate mosaic, varied and colourful. The multitudes of tundra ponds are shallow and reflect the pale northern skies in every shade of blue and violet or, discoloured by organic stains from the muskeg, they become sepia, burnished copper, burning red or shimmering green. The numberless rivers run no straight courses but twist tortuously through chocolate-brown bogs or between silver-grey ridges of stone and gravel (moraines left by the vanished glaciers) or compete in pattern-making with the meandering embankments of sandy eskers (the casts of dead rivers that once flowed under the melting ice sheet). Some eskers roam for hundreds of miles and bear a disconcerting appearance of being the constructions of a long-forgotten race of manic giants.

Viewed by a summer traveller on the ground, the tundra gives the feeling of limitless space, intensified until one wonders if there can be any end to this terrestrial ocean whose waves are the rolling ridges. Perhaps nowhere else in the world, except far out at sea, does a man feel so unconfined. On these northern plains the ceiling of the world seems no longer to exist and no walls close one in.

The climate of these northern prairies – for such they really are – is not very different from that of their southern counterparts. Winter is longer on the tundra but not a great deal colder than on the Saskatchewan plains. Summer is shorter, but the sun shines throughout most of every twenty-four-hour period and during the long summer days the northern plains can become uncomfortably hot. Soil is poor and scanty, but the long summer day makes growth fast and often lush. As on the southern prairies, precipitation, both rain and snow, is light; but in the North where permafrost is everywhere and evaporation slow, this hardly matters since there is little loss of surface water.

Why these mighty plains should ever have been called "barren" is hard to comprehend. Even if the word is only intended to mean treeless, it is not valid. Along the entire southern fringe there are trees, often small and stunted it is true, but trees. And scattered over the southern half of the northern prairies are islands of real timber. One of these, which is on the Thelon River and almost dead centre in the plains, forms a timbered oasis forty or fifty miles in length with some individual trees growing fifty feet in height. If "barren" is intended to mean barren of life, it is also a gross misnomer. True, in winter there is not much life to be seen, but in summer the tundra is vividly alive.

For the most part the land is covered with a rich carpet of mosses, lichens, grasses, sedges and dwarf shrubs. The flowers are small, many of them minute, but they grow in fantastic and colourful abundance. Even on the naked ridges and on the frost-riven jumbles of broken stone that lie between some of the muskeg valleys, there is brilliant life; the rocks glow with the kaleidoscopic splash of lichens in a hundred shades.

Animate life is just as abundant. The innumerable ponds, muskegs and lakes are the breeding grounds for stupendous numbers of ducks, geese and wading birds. The dry tundra and the rock tundra is the habitat of the northern grouse called ptarmigan, and of a good variety of other birds. Snowy owls nest on the grassy flats and rough-legged hawks and falcons share the pale sky with the uncompromising raven which, almost alone among resident arctic animals, refuses to change his colour when winter whiteness obliterates the world. The waters of the larger lakes (those that do not freeze to the bottom in winter) and rivers are full of white fish, lake trout (forty-pounders are not uncommon), suckers and a flamboyant and peculiar fish – a distant relative of the trout – called grayling. Rivers and streams flowing into the sea are home to a luscious relative of the salmon called arctic char.

Insects there are in quantity – a mixed blessing, for although it is pleasant to see butterflies and bumblebees, it is not so pleasant to cope with hordes of mosquitoes and black flies which, particularly in the southern part of the plains, can make life hell on windless days. Fortunately there are few totally windless days in the northern prairies and, in any case, the flies are not a great deal worse than they are in parts of the southern forest regions where urban Canadians delight to spend their summer holidays.

It is the mammals that dominate the land. During the peak period of their population cycles, short-tailed, mouse-like lemmings are so abundant one can hardly walk across the sedge and moss without sending them scuttling clumsily from under foot. They provide the chief food of the white fox whose cycle of abundance is keyed to theirs. Lemmings know nothing about birth control. They breed so prolifically that every four or five years they eat and crowd themselves out of house and home and then must either die or migrate elsewhere – and such migrations are fatal for most of them.

Even squirrels live on the tundra – gaudy, orange-coloured ground squirrels that den in the well-drained sandy eskers or on gravel ridges where the permafrost does not deny them entry.

The great white wolves of the tundra, once abundant but now reduced to a remnant population as the result of federal-supported "control campaigns" using poison bait, display an amiable curiosity, even visiting human campsites to sit with cocked ears as they watch the inscrutable activities of men.

One of the most impressive of all tundra beasts is the great brown Barren-Ground Grizzly. Only a few decades ago, this shambling giant roamed over most of the mainland tundra west of Hudson Bay but, like so many other species that have roused our murderous proclivities, he has become so rare over most of his former range as to be little more than a memory.

Equally strange is the muskox – a black, stolid beast that

looks like a cross between a bull and a shaggy goat (it is distantly related to both). Slow and placid but armed with sweeping horns, muskoxen have evolved the tactic of forming an impenetrable circle when threatened. Because of their fine underlying wool, the wildest winter weather cannot affect them. They have no real enemies save man, and in other times they called almost the entire tundra, both on the mainland and on the islands, home. But by the 1920s they had been almost exterminated. It was chiefly through the persistence of an extraordinary man named W. H. B. Hoare, an ex-missionary who became the champion of the vanishing muskox, that the government in 1927 established a sanctuary for the shaggy beasts in the Thelon Valley. Now the muskoxen are gradually increasing in numbers.

By far the most impressive of all forms of life on the tundra is the caribou. Caribou have literally been the lifeblood of the human residents of the northern plains and of the adjacent taiga since time immemorial. These cousins of the reindeer formerly existed in herds approaching in numbers the buffalo of the southern prairies, and probably outnumbered any of the famous herd beasts of Africa. When Europeans first arrived on the edge of the northern prairie there may have been as many as five million caribou. Caribou and their natural predators, wolves and the native peoples, had lived together in balance for uncounted ages. We changed all that. In 1949, after Ottawa had finally been forced to take notice of the terrible destruction of these northern deer, an aerial survey showed that only about 650,000 remained alive. By 1955 their number was estimated to be 280,000. By 1960 there were fewer than 200,000, most of them west of Hudson Bay. In the Ungava Barrens the caribou had become so scarce by the early 1950s that it was predicted they would be extinct there by the end of that decade. It is only fair to add that the slide toward extinction seems now to have been halted and even reversed.

The fur trade was the major influence in destroying the caribou. It turned the northern peoples from hunting the animals for their own use to destroying them wholesale for bait and dog food so they could trap more efficiently. Very large numbers of caribou were also killed annually to provide the northern fur brigades of the trading companies with the travel food called pemmican. High-powered repeating rifles accomplished what thousands of years of bow and arrow, deer corrals, spearing at river crossings, snaring, poor fawning seasons and wolves had not been able to do – they broke the balance. The destruction was greatly assisted by white trappers, some of whom killed as many as four hundred caribou a year for bait and dog food; and by white prospectors for minerals who deliberately burned off millions of acres of caribou winter range inside the taiga in order to expose the native rock beneath. Man-made forest fires have been a primary reason for the decimation of the herds in the Quebec-Labrador Peninsula.

The destruction of the caribou went forward on the same scale as the destruction of the prairie buffalo. As late as 1900 the northern deer had still been so abundant that herds which could only be described in terms of square miles still existed. There is a reliable record of a single herd seen in 1897 that consisted of more than two hundred thousand individuals.

When Samuel Hearne crossed the tundra plains from Churchill to the Coppermine River in the 1770s, he found several thousand Indians in the taiga-tundra meeting ground living exclusively on caribou. When explorers J. B. and J. W. Tyrrell traversed Keewatin in 1893 there were still several hundreds of Eskimos in the interior plains who did not visit the sea coast and were exclusively a people of the deer. In Ungava, between 1830 and 1900, the Naskapi Indians of the interior, and many Eskimos as well, led lives largely predicated on caribou. Yet by 1966 in the whole vast stretch of interior Keewatin there was *not one* resident Indian or Eskimo except at the single settlement of Baker Lake. The interior tundra of northern Quebec and the inland tundra regions of the Mackenzie District were also devoid of native peoples. The many and varied peoples of the deer across the breadth of the northern Canadian plains had vanished with the caribou. Only a handful of the inland Eskimos still survive, most of them huddling in wooden shacks at Eskimo Point and Baker Lake where they live mainly on relief. Less than a thousand taiga Indians, of the tens of thousands who once depended on the extensive caribou herds which used to winter south of the tree line, still exist, in desperate poverty around dying trading posts in the border forests of northern Saskatchewan and Manitoba.

Whites never effectively occupied the northern prairies they had despoiled. Indeed, they hardly even explored them before the advent of the airplane. The northern plains saw few white visitors until the late 1920s – apart from the Royal Navy's Captain George Back, who in 1834 descended the river that now bears his name; J. B. and J. W. Tyrrell, who between 1892 and 1900 canoed the Dubawnt, Kazan and Thelon rivers; and a few wanderers such as John Hornby, who in 1927 left his bones and those of two companions in the Thelon oasis. But when white fox fur became fashionable and reached a peak value, traders crowded to the edge of the tundra and even pushed a short distance into it to compete with one another for the furs trapped by Eskimos and Indians. The traders were followed, or were sometimes led, by a handful of misanthropic Whites who were collectively known as the Barren-Ground trappers and who chiefly relied on strychnine instead of traps. By 1950, coincidentally with the last days of the Caribou Eskimos, most of these trappers and all the traders had withdrawn from the land. Today an occasional aircraft drones overhead. Now and again a prospecting crew descends on some silent lake. For the rest, nearly half a million square miles of Canada lie vacant.

It need not be abandoned. It should not be. Where once millions of caribou prospered, meat-producing animals could again make it possible for the native peoples to repopulate the northern prairies. It has been done in Siberia, Lapland, even in Alaska, and it could be done here. Reindeer,

91

herded and semi-domesticated, or wild muskox and caribou carefully husbanded, could bring new life to this empty land. The world is short of meat, which will become even scarcer. Even now, more than half the world's population is starving for protein. *We* may be well fed on steaks and roast beef but we are the exception. Deliberately pessimistic reports, many by government employees, have been written to prove that the northern prairies cannot produce any significant amount of meat for human use, and that Eskimos and Indians are unable, and unwilling, to learn to become herders. These time-serving reports are given the lie both by what the tundra *did* produce in the past and by what the tundra regions of Scandinavia and Siberia *are* producing today. Perhaps an explanation of these gloomy prophecies can be found in what happened in Alaska. There, during the 1920s, the Lomen brothers were instrumental in building up herds of reindeer totalling over two hundred thousand animals. Many of these belonged to Eskimos, and still more Eskimos were employed with the Lomen herds. The intention was to supply high-quality, low-cost meat to the main body of the United States. When the first shipments reached California they created a sensation among a population avid to buy – and created near-panic among western cattle and sheep ranchers who began loudly lobbying Washington, demanding that the new competitor be curbed. Washington responded by expropriating the Lomen herds and by imposing an embargo on the export of reindeer meat from Alaska. Deprived of southern markets, the herds shrank away to a remnant population of about 20,000 animals – not even sufficient to supply local needs; and scores of Eskimo families who had begun to build new lives based on reindeer herding went on the dole.

It is reasonably certain that something similar happened in the Canadian North, where reindeer have twice been introduced. The first attempt was made on Baffin Island in the early 1920s when Vilhjalmur Stefansson persuaded the Hudson's Bay Company to lease a huge area in the southern part of the island and stock it with reindeer. The experiment would probably have succeeded if the Company had persevered. It did not do so partly owing to management difficulties, and the preliminary herd soon went wild.

The second experiment was far more important. In 1929 the Government of Canada purchased a herd from the Lomen brothers in Alaska and had it driven to the Mackenzie River Delta – a fantastic trek that took five years to complete. Once arrived in the Delta the herd should have increased quickly and new herds ought to have been established from it right across the Canadian North – that having been the original intention. That this did not happen seems to have been due to a sudden but never-explained loss of interest by the federal authorities, who seem to have run into the same sort of opposition from southern ranchers that the Alaskan experiment had experienced. In any event neglect gradually wasted the herd until March, 1974, when the remnants were sold by the Canadian Wildlife Service to an Eskimo, Silas Kangegana, who is now busily demonstrating that Eskimos can and do make excellent herdsmen, and that reindeer husbandry in the Far North is eminently practicable and can be economically successful. In June of 1976 the first shipments of reindeer meat to southern Canada from Silas Kangegana's herd went on sale in Edmonton and Vancouver. In both cities the shipments, consisting of some 21,000 lbs., were sold out within a day at prices ranging from 89 cents a pound for ground meat to $1.99 for sirloin tip roasts.

The value of reindeer husbandry has been amply demonstrated during the past several decades in Sweden, Norway, Finland and, particularly, in the U.S.S.R. where by the end of 1975 there was a base herd of two million reindeer, which in that year produced better than 30,000 tons of meat, large quantities of chamois leather and more than a hundred by-products, including glandular extracts for medicinal use. The Soviet reindeer industry provides steady, relatively high-income employment to more than ten thousand mostly indigenous peoples (including many of the U.S.S.R.'s Eskimos), which would represent a good proportion of the *entire* native population of Canada's North.

Dr. V. N. Andreyev, winner of a Lenin Prize for his reindeer research, has visited northern Canada and agrees with Finnish experts that the carrying capacity of the Canadian Arctic is in excess of two million domesticated reindeer, even allowing for a considerable increase in the size of native caribou herds. In 1973 I was involved in bringing two Soviet reindeer specialists to northern Manitoba to conduct a feasibility survey there. They reported that the tundra plains of southern and central Keewatin, combined with the taiga wintering range in Manitoba, could easily support from twenty-two to forty herds of from four to six thousand domesticated reindeer each, without seriously interfering with the caribou. The Manitoba government is anxious to implement this report but cannot do so without the co-operation of the government of the Northwest Territories, which means in effect the federal government. There is no indication that such co-operation will ever be forthcoming.

Another practical suggestion is muskox husbandry. These animals scarcely need to be herded since they ramble very slowly across the tundra. Their meat is excellent and their undercoat is made of a wool-like material finer than cashmere, and which is worth more than its weight in gold. The wild caribou herds themselves, once restored to something approaching their original numbers, could be systematically cropped by native co-operatives not only to provide food for the North but also export products which could earn good incomes for the native peoples involved – not just for a few years but in perpetuity.

The only official explanation I have been able to uncover as to why animal husbandry has not been encouraged in the North is that it would not be "economically viable." On analysis this turns out to mean that there would be little likelihood of quick and easy profits for those who believe the

North exists primarily to be exploited by Southerners.

At a time when the majority of Eskimos and northern Indians have no meaningful work or sustaining means of livelihood, this immense expanse of arctic prairie could provide many of them with an opportunity to recover pride of self, to find freedom from the dole and to build new lives in the only world with which they are familiar and at home. Such work would certainly be more in keeping with their approach to life than working on pipeline construction or deep in the dark shafts of mines.

"In the springtime when the ice moves we used to see lots of ducks and hear the birds sing. We don't hear that anymore."
Mary Husky, Aklavik

"If the government give the land to the native people for their children in the future, I will be very happy."
William Nerysoo, Fort McPherson

"We worry about the pipeline, not for us old people but for our younger generation. We worry about what is going to happen to our land."
Lucy Vaneltsi,
Fort McPherson

"I play fiddle for people. I go all around here to play fiddle. I'm good . . . but I used to be better."
Alfred Bernard,
Fort McPherson

"In our heads we thank Judge Berger for listening to our voices."
Martha Stewart, Aklavik

Ivy Kowikchuk of Tuktoyaktuk looks to the future of the New North with foreboding.

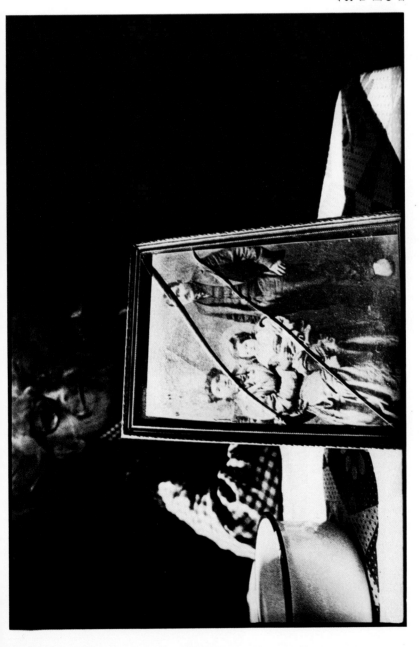

At Aklavik, Andrew Stewart remembers the days of his parents and his own childhood with nostalgia.

The strength of a people is the strength of its women. Rebecca Modest and Lucy Francis of Fort McPherson.

"If you ask any of the Eskimos here if they agree with the drilling out in the Beaufort Sea, every one of them say 'No!'"
Emmanuel Felix, Tuktoyaktuk

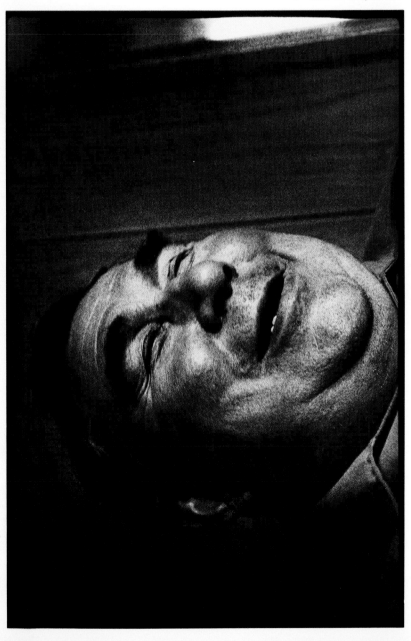

"One time we always got lots of fish in the lakes but it really changed since the oil companies come . . . . all that blasting killed so much fish."
Raddi Kowikchuk, Tuktoyaktuk

"We try to teach our kids to live off the land. They like going to the bush. But after our land is destroyed there will be nothing to take them out there for."
ex-Chief John Charlie, Fort McPherson

Each spring scores of Eskimo, Métis and Indian families disperse throughout the Mackenzie Delta for the annual muskrat hunt.

The alternative.
The New North
of Northern
Development . . . .
Main street
of Fort McPherson.

Collins Harry and his youngest son, Kenneth, enjoy what may be the closing days of a vanishing way of life . . . living off the land.

Ratting amidst the dissolving ice of one of the Mackenzie Delta's countless channels. Walter and Kenneth Harry.

Collins Harry and his family look forward to the spring "ratting"—the muskrat hunt—as the one really vital element left to them in a world full of bewildering change.

VII

The Islands in the Ice

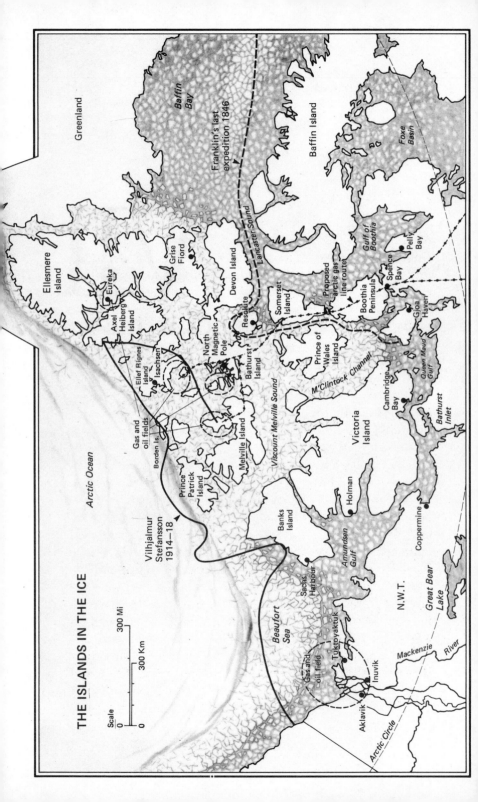

THE ISLANDS IN THE ICE

Scale

0   300 Mi

0   300 Km

Greenland

Baffin Bay

Franklin's last expedition 1846

Baffin Island

Foxe Basin

Ellesmere Island

Grise Fiord

Devon Island

Lancaster Sound

Gulf of Boothia

Pelly Bay

Eureka

Axel Heiberg Island

North Magnetic Pole

Resolute

Somerset Island

Proposed arctic gas line route

Spence Bay

Boothia Peninsula

Gioa Haven

Ellef Rignes Island

Isachsen

Bathurst Island

Prince of Wales Island

Queen Maud Gulf

Gas and oil fields

Borden Is.

Melville Island

M'Clintock Channel

Cambridge Bay

Bathurst Inlet

Viscount Melville Sound

Prince Patrick Island

Vilhjalmur Stefansson 1914–18

Arctic Ocean

Victoria Island

Holman

Banks Island

Coppermine

Sachs Harbour

Amundsen Gulf

Great Bear Lake

N.W.T.

Beaufort Sea

Gas and oil field

Tuktoyaktuk

Inuvik

Mackenzie River

Aklavik

Arctic Circle

Mainland Canada's northwest coast is not, as some may think, the coast of northern British Columbia – it is the shoreline of the Arctic Ocean which runs fourteen hundred miles, as the raven flies, east and west between the Alaska-Yukon border and Foxe Basin on the Canadian Sea. This coast bounds Yukon Territory and the Districts of Mackenzie and Keewatin on the north, but it also forms the southern base for a huge, slanting pyramid of islands that thrusts its apex toward the Pole.

The islands are separated from the mainland by a chain of waterways that most Canadians do not even know exist – including Amundsen Gulf, Dolphin and Union Strait, Coronation Gulf, Dease Strait, Queen Maud Gulf, Simpson Strait and the Gulf of Boothia. These waterways are usually ice-free in summer and so they provide a natural transportation route along the top of the continent. The island shores to the north of them, and the mainland shores to the south, were once among the most heavily populated areas in the Canadian Arctic. The western reaches belonged to the Mackenzie Eskimos, the central area to the Copper Eskimos, and the eastern regions to the Netsilik Eskimos. The latter were the last of their race to be wrenched away from the old verities of Eskimo life and thrust into the uncertainties of the modern world.

Although the northwest Arctic coast was glimpsed by Hearne in 1771 at the mouth of the Coppermine River, and by Mackenzie in 1789 at the mouth of the river named for

115

him, other interlopers were slow to follow. Not until the end of the nineteenth century did Yankee whalers poke their noses around Point Barrow in Alaska and begin killing whales and other sea mammals in the Beaufort Sea, using Herschel Island as a base. Not until 1910 did Vilhjalmur Stefansson make the first real contact between Whites and the Copper Eskimos; and not until after the First World War did traders filter eastward into the Netsilik country.

During the 1920s the connecting series of waterways along the northwest coast became an avenue of riches for the traders. Since it is a blind avenue (its eastward end is blocked by northward-thrusting Boothia Peninsula) trade goods flowed into it and furs flowed out either around Alaska or via the Mackenzie River. At the start of the White-Gold Rush (as the exploitation of the white fox was called) the northern shores were still occupied by an almost continuous frieze of small Eskimo settlements. Today the Eskimos who survived the invasion of the twenties are clotted into a few widely separated communities.

Pelly Bay, the settlement farthest to the east, in the Gulf of Boothia, is a special case. Because it had no usable sea communication with the northern waterway *or* with Hudson Bay, it continued to exist in virtual isolation from White contact until an Oblate mission was established there in 1933. It remains one of the more viable Eskimo communities due partly to its comparative isolation, but mainly to the abundance of "country meat" in the form of sea mammals and caribou in a region where these were never unduly exploited.

The two hundred or so Pelly Bay people have formed an effective co-operative which runs the local store and a handicraft centre, and is also the backbone of the Federation of Arctic Co-operatives which the Eskimos have been struggling to establish across the Arctic in opposition to southern commercial interests.

Westward from Pelly Bay lies Spence Bay, a non-community whose location was arbitrarily chosen by the Royal Canadian Mounted Police and the Hudson's Bay Company in a poor hunting area. The majority of the Netsilik (Seal People) from the east-central Arctic now cluster at Spence Bay where they are provided with wooden houses, schools and medical attention – but with no way to make a satisfactory living. Westward again, on King William Island, lies Gjoa Haven. Here the story is much the same as at Spence although a small proportion of the people still find a limited occupation in seal hunting and fox trapping. Still farther west, on Victoria Island, is Cambridge Bay, which is another Frobisher Bay in miniature. It boasts a Distant-Early-Warning-Line site and a large modern airport. The white population consists mainly of government employees overseeing some seven hundred Eskimos, many of whom have passed through the new school system but have no opportunity to use their newly acquired education.

On the mainland, near the mouth of Bathurst Inlet, there is one small community which has so far resisted the centralization program. In 1976 seventy-five Eskimos still lived at Bay Chimo in a traditional camp without benefit of northern administrators, trading post, police, teachers or even a resident nurse. They lived by choice *on* the land and *from* it, and were a vigorous, self-reliant and effective group. It remains to be seen how long they can hold out.

Two other communities farther west, Holman on the shore of Victoria Island, and Sachs Harbour on Banks Island, are also notable because of the stubborn refusal of their people to be moulded into imitation Whites. The people at Sachs Harbour are the most prosperous natives in the North, and they have become so by learning how to deal with Whites on White terms while retaining their native allegiance to the land. They treat Banks Island as a huge fur farm for white fox, reap a carefully controlled crop each year and protect this renewable resource from being depleted. When oil exploration companies tried to run roughshod over the island, the Sachs people reacted so vigorously that the authorities were forced to limit the oil men's activities.

*   *   *

The Canadian Arctic archipelago is divided naturally into two parallel tiers separated from each other by Parry Channel which runs east and west through Lancaster Sound, Viscount Melville Sound and M'Clure Strait, between Baffin Bay and the Beaufort Sea.

The lower tier, facing the mainland coast, includes Banks, Victoria, King William, Prince of Wales and Somerset islands, as well as Boothia and Melville peninsulas – which are peninsulas only in the narrowest technical sense, being joined to the mainland by very narrow isthmuses, as a nearly severed leg may be joined to the body. Baffin Island also belongs to the lower tier.

Victoria and Banks islands, separated from each other by the narrow Prince of Wales Strait and from the mainland by equally narrow waters, are as big as the entire British Isles. Together with Prince of Wales and King William islands they form an extension of the northern prairies and share the same kind of rolling tundra. Low and monotonous when seen from the air, they too show an amazing richness on the ground.

The straits separating these islands from the mainland freeze solidly during the winter, and as a result these several islands are firmly joined to the mainland for as much as eight months of the year. Great herds of caribou once used to treat the islands of the lower tier as part of the mainland, migrating northward to them by the hundreds of thousands over the ice in late spring, and returning southward again in the late autumn. These migratory herds have now vanished, but remnants of them still live on the islands all year round, together with a few thousand muskoxen.

The eastern portion of the lower tier, Somerset Island and the Boothia and Melville peninsulas, has a different nature. Much more rugged and bony, the land is cleft with ancient valleys and studded with rounded hills. Nevertheless this region too once harboured considerable herds of caribou and muskoxen.

The waters around all the islands of the lower tier were

rich in seals, white whales and Greenland Right Whales until these were decimated by whaling fleets and by the demands made on them in connection with the fur trade. Properly managed, and protected from the dangers of massive hydrocarbon pollution, their populations could again build to a level where they could not only feed the surviving Eskimos of the coastal regions but could provide the basis for a sustaining economy as well.

Not long ago Eskimos occupied all the islands of the lower tier, as their numerous abandoned settlement sites still testify. Europeans first came to these islands in 1819-20 when Parry went sailing west down the great channel which now bears his name, almost completing the Northwest Passage. James Clark Ross explored Boothia Peninsula and Somerset Island between 1829 and 1833 while with an expedition commanded by his uncle, John Ross, and located the North Magnetic Pole on Boothia. But Boothia has since lost the honour, for the North Magnetic Pole is a wanderer and by 1976 lay hidden under the waters of Viscount Melville Sound. Victoria Island was first seen, from the south, by Sir John Franklin's second overland expedition in 1825-27. East of this island Franklin's grandiose Northwest Passage expedition of 1845-48, consisting of two fine ships, was beset north of King William Island and 129 officers and men vanished into death and darkness. Only fragmentary details of that tragedy have been recovered by the dozens of expeditions that have searched the lower tier from east, west and south, scouring it for traces of the missing voyagers. Apparently the two ships got as far as Victoria Strait, between King William and Victoria islands, where they were trapped in the ice during the winter of 1846. Franklin died the next year and his second-in-command, Crozier, took over. In 1848 Crozier and his men abandoned the imprisoned ships and, dragging heavy oaken boats over the ice, began a hopeless trek southward along the coast of King William Island. Singly at first, then in groups, the sailors died of scurvy and starvation. A few exceptionally tough individuals got as far

119

as an islet in Chantry Inlet on the mainland coast, where their greening bones were discovered long years afterwards. The story of Franklin's last expedition is one of horror. It need not have been. Its men and officers seem to have been so convinced that Europeans could not live from the land that they stuck to scurvy-producing canned and dried foods brought from home while ignoring the abundance of fresh meat available around them which could have sustained them in good health as it was then sustaining a large population of Netsilik Eskimos.

A few Netsilik people still hunt on eastern Melville and southern Boothia peninsulas, King William Island and the south shores of Victoria and Banks islands; but the great hinterland, an area of nearly a hundred thousand square miles of tundra, is, like the tundra of the mainland, now devoid of all human inhabitants.

The upper island tier of the archipelago is a different land with a different story. Now called the Queen Elizabeth Islands, it forms the top of the triangle and includes Prince Patrick, Melville, Bathurst, Cornwallis, Cornwall, Amund Ringnes, Ellef Ringnes, Meighen, Mackenzie King, Borden, Brock, Devon, Axel Heiberg, Ellesmere and a number of smaller islands which together occupy about two hundred thousand square miles of land and water. Axel Heiberg and Ellesmere together with eastern Devon are part of the Icy Mountains. The remainder of these islands, except those facing south on the Parry Channel, were until recently among the most inaccessible lands on earth. Some of them, including Mackenzie King, Borden, Meighen and Lougheed, had remained unknown until Stefansson discovered them between 1914 and 1918.

Parts of the Queen Elizabeth Islands contain exposed portions of a vast, largely submerged, coastal plain. The extreme north-central islands have only recently (in geological time) emerged from the sea and are still rising. They tend to be flat, low and formless and most are perpetually surrounded by polar ice. Plant life is scanty; sedges, mosses and tiny flowering plants struggle against a stern climate for survival. Nevertheless, all of the larger islands of the upper tier, except perhaps Meighen, once supported healthy herds of caribou and muskoxen and most retain small residual herds today. Seals of several species thrive in the waters surrounding the southeastern portions of the Queen Elizabeth Islands, keeping in touch with the upper world by gnawing breathing holes through the ice cover. Narwhals and walrus are found in some localities in the southeastern parts of the Queen Elizabeth Islands, and polar bears roam wherever there are seals. Although some recent publicity by oil exploration companies gives the impression that these islands comprise a useless and uninhabitable desert, the fact is that Stefansson and his party travelled for many months and covered thousands of miles through this region living almost exclusively on the natural produce of land and sea. Archaeology has also shown that most of the region was formerly hunted over, and much of it was occupied by Eskimos.

Today there are only three "permanent" clusters of humanity to be found in the upper tier. Two of these are the remote weather stations of Eureka on Ellesmere Island and Isachsen on Ellef Ringnes Island. But they do not constitute real settlements so much as embattled outposts of technology.

Resolute Bay on Cornwallis Island is the only settlement deserving of the name. Since its prime function is to provide an advanced base for oil, gas and mineral exploration of the high Arctic islands, it has become a boom town. The federal government is building a new townsite there at an estimated cost of 7.5 million dollars mainly to house and service the transient white population, but incidentally to provide for the hundred or so Eskimos who live there permanently.

Fossil fuel is the focus of attention in the Queen Elizabeth group. Oil and gas exploration permits covering almost all of the archipelago and its associated waterways have already been issued. Wildcat drilling began in the early seventies and by 1974 oil had been found under Ellef Ringnes and Ellesmere, and immense coal fields are believed to underlie other islands. But the finds that really fuelled the boom were three major gas fields discovered under Melville, King Christian, Thor and Ellef Ringnes islands and the intervening channels. Exploitation of these fields promises tremendous profits but also poses hideous risks to the environment. These were all-too-brilliantly illuminated when the first two wells to strike gas – one on King Christian Island and the other on Melville Island – *both* blew out of control. They burned with volcanic heat and smoke for many weeks before finally being capped. The dangers were increased manifold in 1974 when Panarctic began winter drilling under the waterways of the Sverdrup Basin using rigs positioned on artificially constructed ice islands. Even Panarctic experts admitted it might take as much as a year before an underwater blowout in such a well could be controlled. That the danger is indeed very real was demonstrated during the winter of 1975 when ice movement caused one of the artificial ice platforms to shift and a partially drilled hole had to be hurriedly abandoned. Although not as dangerous as an oil blowout, an underwater gas blowout could be expected to release tons of highly toxic hydrocarbons into the waters. These would spell death to all aquatic life within a wide radius of the well. A recently tested sample of oil from the Sverdrup Basin showed a high sulphur content. This means that hydrocarbons from this basin will likely be especially toxic because of the presence of hydrogen sulphide.

As has been the case with all offshore drilling programs in the Canadian North, only the most superficial efforts have been made to assess the environmental effects which would result from an accident. Neither the oil companies nor any federal government agencies have made more than token gestures toward properly evaluating the potential dangers to land, air and water, and to both human and non-human life. For the most part, their public protestations of concern have consisted of empty rhetoric. It seems abundantly clear that both government and industry are prepared to accept the probability of major disasters in their anxiety to exploit these discoveries.

An even more frightening prospect for the future of the islands is a proposal by Norlands, a subsidiary of Northern Natural Gas (Nebraska, U.S.A.), to drill wildcat wells for both oil and gas under Lancaster Sound. This mighty waterway is the principal channel in the archipelago and is particularly rich in marine life ranging from microscopic plankton to sixty-foot Greenland Right Whales, a few of which – having escaped the earlier massacre – now represent the last hope for the survival of their species.

Lancaster Sound is tremendously deep and Norlands will have to drill in water depths of up to three thousand feet, which will be much deeper than has ever been attempted anywhere in the world. Considering the unpredictable movement of heavy ice through the Sound, as well as the great depth of drill-in-water, it is obvious that the odds favouring an accident which could result in a blowout are intolerably high. Nevertheless, indications are that Norlands or some other foreign company will soon receive permission "to engage in a risk venture" in Lancaster Sound. The drilling company's risk will be financial only. The real and present risk of major damage to the Arctic islands and surrounding seas will be borne by Canada.

There are other problems. By mid-1976 proven finds of gas in the archipelago were nearly large enough to make a pipeline to the south appear financially attractive. Despite a preliminary cost estimate in excess of ten billion dollars for construction, a consortium calling itself Polar Gas was already preparing an application to the National Energy Board of Canada for permission to build such a line from island to island, running under the many channels to the mainland of Boothia Peninsula, after which it would run south down the west or east coast of Hudson Bay, with the likelihood that the west side would be chosen. Unless the underwater portions are placed in a tunnel, the dangers posed to such a pipeline by deep bottom scouring from thickly raftered sections of pack ice (ditches twenty feet deep have been found on the bottom of the Beaufort Sea resulting from such scouring) are so severe that breaks in the line might well become annual events. Furthermore, once the line reaches the mainland, it is slated to pass close to the Eskimo settlements of Spence Bay, Pelly Bay and Baker Lake with consequences which are likely to be as disastrous to the people of those communities as to the great stretch of arctic prairie through which the line will pass.

Because of their distance from the South, and their small human population, the islands in the ice are being treated with an almost total disregard for consequences. Neither the government agencies involved nor the oil consortiums seem concerned that their activities in this "arctic desert" (as one oil company has publicly labelled the region) will spark any effective opposition from Southerners. As one senior oil company executive puts it:

> "People down south have got to have the hydrocarbons. They want them and they want them badly. It's going to be no skin off their noses if we have to mess things up a little bit up there to get them what they want. Nobody is going to give much of a damn as long as we deliver the goods. Why should they? They [the islands] are away back of nowhere and they aren't worth anything to anybody anyhow. At least *we* plan to give them some real hard-cash value!"

Although the fate of Canada's islands in the ice – and indeed of the rest of the North – currently rests in the hands of men in industry and government who think in these terms, it may not always remain so. If it does not, it will be with no thanks to southern Canadians – the credit will belong to the native people of the North.

In March, 1976, Inuit Tapirisat (The Eskimo Brotherhood) representing the fifteen thousand Eskimos of the

Northwest Territories (but not, alas, those in Quebec) presented the federal cabinet with an offer to settle the land claims dispute. It was a remarkable offer.

Having first established their aboriginal rights to some 750,000 square miles of arctic territory encompassing almost the whole of the tundra regions, on the basis of immemorial occupancy and use, the Eskimos then offered to make *a free gift of half a million square miles of their ancestral lands to the Crown* – the remaining quarter of a million square miles to be retained as Eskimo property.

As the representatives of Inuit Tapirisat carefully pointed out to Prime Minister Trudeau and his colleagues:

"We are not asking anything from you. We are not asking for land or for money or for anything at all. It is *we* who are offering to give Canada two-thirds of *our* lands in exchange for some considerations which will never cost the Canadian taxpayer a single cent."

These considerations are, first, that the Eskimos shall retain exclusive hunting, fishing and trapping rights in perpetuity over the entire territory, which is to be called Nunavut – Our Land. Second, the Eskimos are to receive a three per cent royalty on the profits of all mining and other resource developments which take place in the 500,000 square miles deeded to Canada. This money will be held in common in an Inuit Development Corporation and used to repair the social damages suffered by the Eskimos under Canadian rule and to fund projects upon which an economy tuned to Eskimo needs and inclinations can be built. The third major condition of the gift is that the Eskimos reserve to themselves a watchdog role in order to ensure that all development is undertaken with due regard for the preservation of the environment. They are particularly concerned about the future of the arctic prairies for it has not escaped their notice that these broad plains have a tremendous potential for animal husbandry, be it wild caribou, semi-domesticated muskox or domesticated reindeer.

The spokesmen for the Brotherhood concluded their presentation by expressing the hope that eventually the territory will become the Province of Nunavut in which Southerners and Eskimos can live and work together in amity and with equality. They made it clear that they have no inclination to secede. They reiterated that they wish to be Canadians but they insisted that they must be allowed to share the rights and rewards as well as the obligations which such citizenship entails.

The reaction of the Trudeau cabinet was polite but noncommital, yet it is hard to see how even a colonially oriented government could justify turning down such a generous offer and, moreover, one which is manifestly in the best interests of both southern and northern Canadians – although certainly not in the best interests of the international resource exploitation corporations.

There have been some straws in the wind to suggest how the federal government will deal with the offer. Although he had earlier promised Inuit Tapirisat that he would impose a moratorium on new "resource development" projects in the proposed Nunavut territory until settlement of the land claims issue had been reached, Indian Affairs and Northern Development Minister Judd Buchanan did not keep that agreement. Barely two weeks after Inuit Tapirisat had presented its brief to cabinet, Mr. Buchanan announced that he had granted as many as sixty permits to companies wishing to immediately begin prospecting for uranium in Keewatin, which is the very heartland of the Nunavut territory. The Eskimos can have little hope that Mr. Buchanan, who is in effect the overlord of the Northwest Territories on behalf of the federal government, will throw *his* support behind their offer.

Eskimo people held stewardship over the tundra regions of Canada North for some thousands of years before the coming of Europeans, and they did not abuse that stewardship. Surely it would be well for us, for the North, for the world we all live in, if we returned it to their safekeeping.

"It is not for ourselves we are willing to fight to keep our land alive. It is for our children and their children we will fight!"
A Dene spokesman

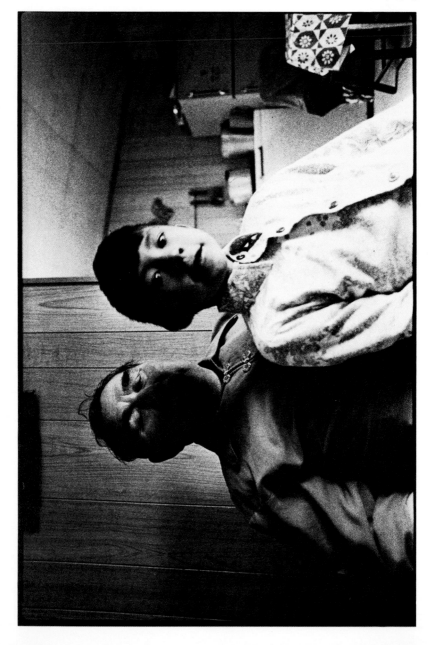

Raddi Kowikchuk
with his grandson,
Christopher Raddi,
of Tuktoyaktuk.

Maureen Chicksi of
Tuktoyaktuk.

Arnold, Christopher and Trevor Raddi of Tuktoyaktuk.

Francis Anderson and Darren Nogasak of Tuktoyaktuk.

Most Inuit want their kids to know the inner certainty and pride they felt themselves. *We* want them to grow up as Whites . . . . Ruined lives in a ruined world!''
A government employee at Yellowknife

Bertha Chicksi of
Tuktoyaktuk.

Fred Jacobson of
Tuktoyaktuk.

Richard Gordon of
Aklavik.

"We see movies about wars between Whites and Indians and every time the Indians always lose. I ask the people of southern Canada to let us win this one."
Charlie Furlong,
Aklavik

Walter Harry of
Aklavik.

"Our way of life will change, but let us do it in our own time . . . in our own way."
Spokesman for The Eskimo Brotherhood addressing Prime Minister Trudeau and his cabinet.

VIII

The Western Highland

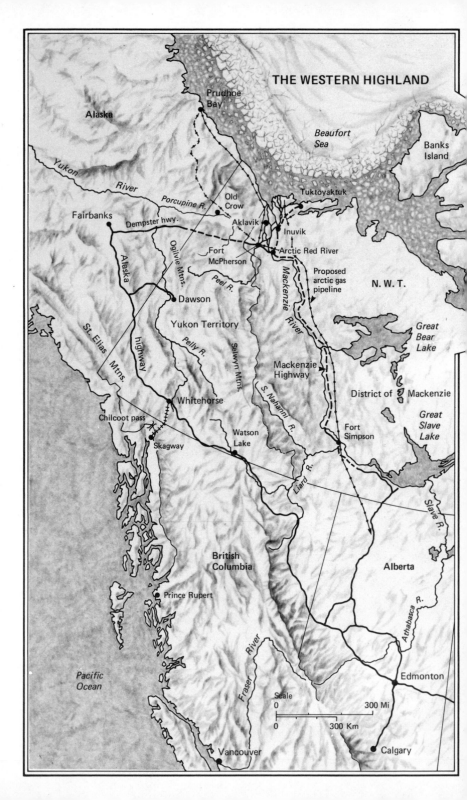

THE WESTERN HIGHLAND

Alaska

Prudhoe Bay

Beaufort Sea

Banks Island

Yukon River

Porcupine R.

Old Crow

Tuktoyaktuk

Fairbanks

Dempster hwy.

Aklavik

Inuvik

Arctic Red River

N. W. T.

Fort McPherson

Peel R.

Proposed arctic gas pipeline

Mackenzie River

Alaska highway

Ogilvie Mtns.

Dawson

Yukon Territory

Pelly R.

Selwyn Mtns.

Great Bear Lake

St. Elias Mtns.

Mackenzie Highway

District of Mackenzie

Great Slave Lake

Whitehorse

Chilcoot pass

Watson Lake

S. Nahanni R.

Fort Simpson

Skagway

Liard R.

Slave R.

British Columbia

Alberta

Prince Rupert

Fraser River

Athabasca R.

Pacific Ocean

Scale

0   300 Mi

0   300 Km

Edmonton

Vancouver

Calgary

Tucked away in the northwestern corner of Canada lies a very special country. Although it is somewhat smaller and less formidable than Tibet (and boasts no lamas), the two regions have their similarities. The Western Highland is an up-thrust, roughly triangular block of ancient folded mountains consisting of a quarter million square miles of peaks, plateaus, glaciers, canyons, tundra plains and broad, mountain-guarded river valleys. Four-fifths of this massive block goes to make up Yukon Territory; the remainder forms a bulbous projection pushing eastward into the District of Mackenzie.

On its eastern verges the Western Highland rises in a series of gigantic steps beginning with the Canyon Ranges whose feet stand almost in the waters of the Mackenzie River. The Canyons are deeply slashed by harshly sculptured valleys savagely cut by roaring rivers like the Mountain, Keele, Twitya, Redstone and, most dramatic of all, the South Nahanni. This river, with its limestone pinnacles, sunless clefts, fantastic cliffs, and appalling rapids, has exercised a baleful influence on most white men who have seen it. No other region in Canada has accumulated such a dark mythology: semi-human monsters who behead intruders; madness that overwhelms strangers; lost gold mines that promise death to those who stumble on them; hot-spring valleys filled with tropical vegetation and tropical beasts. The myths are only myths, but the reality is impressive enough. Rising below peaks nine thousand feet high, the South Nahanni

147

River rages southeastward to the Liard, at one point thundering over Virginia Falls in a drop of 316 feet.

Beyond the Canyon Ranges loom the Backbone Ranges, dominated in their turn by the magnificent, glacier-encrusted Selwyn Mountains whose peaks reach to more than ten thousand feet. The Selwyns form the top of the wall – to the west lie the Yukon Plateau, Peel Plateau and Porcupine Plain, divided from one another and bisected and traversed by mountain massifs.

The Yukon Plateau is by far the largest. It is walled off from its two northern neighbours by the brooding Ogilvie Mountains; cut off from the Pacific Ocean by the St. Elias Mountains (whose mighty peaks, lancing up through a vast glacier complex, reach over twenty thousand feet), and from British Columbia to the south by the northern buttresses of the Cassiar and Coastal ranges.

The Peel Plateau and Porcupine Plain between them occupy the Western Highland north of the Ogilvie Mountains and are themselves walled in on the east by the Richardson Mountains, and on the north (almost at the Arctic coast) by the British Mountains. The Porcupine and Yukon plateaus extend westward to occupy much of central Alaska; but this is alien soil. Here is the one place where Canada's North borders directly on a foreign country.

Each of the three highland plateaus is drained by a river bearing its name. The Peel River is an oddity, for it flows eastward through a gap between the Richardson and Selwyn mountains to join the Mackenzie River. The Porcupine, lying farthest north, flows westward into Alaska where it eventually becomes part of the mighty Yukon, which is North America's third longest river. Although some of the headwaters of the Yukon rise in British Columbia within fifteen miles of tide-water on the Pacific Ocean, it empties into Alaska's Norton Sound on the Bering Sea after running a course of more than twenty-two hundred miles! Except for its upper reaches it is navigable to shallow-draft vessels, and much of the system offers superb canoe routes. It is an ancient river, much older than the St. Lawrence or the Mackenzie, for it alone of all the major rivers of the North was not obliterated, reshaped or redirected during the last great glaciation. The titanic ice sheet that covered most of Canada and spread far south into the United States stopped short about halfway across the Western Highland, leaving part of the Yukon and Porcupine basins untouched, an "oasis" which escaped the ice age. Here relict populations of now-extinct beasts, including the mammoth and the mastodon, survived long after most members of their species elsewhere had been overwhelmed.

Because of its antiquity the Yukon River has had ample time to wear down the ancient barriers that must once have obstructed its passage with innumerable falls and rapids, and so it had become a natural and easy highway for humans during inter-glacial periods as long as thirty thousand years ago. Some of the earliest immigrants to North America from Asia ascended the broad waterway of the Yukon into and through the maze of interior mountains. From the headwaters of the Porcupine they crossed McDougall Pass, the lowest elevation (1,000 feet) in the whole Rocky Mountain system, to the Peel and descended it to the Mackenzie which they ascended to the forests of what is now northern Alberta.

In our age men have gone the other way. Although Hudson's Bay Company explorers ascended the Liard River in the 1820s and explored part of the Yukon River in the 1840s, it was not until 1883 that Lieutenant Frederick Schwatka of the U.S. Army followed the Yukon all the way down to its distant mouth.

The ice sheet that rasped the rest of the Canadian North not only spared many of the rivers of the Western Highland but the land as well, so that the face of much of the country went unscathed. It is an incredibly ancient face, aged by the imperceptibly slow processes of water and wind erosion. An aura of unimaginable antiquity lies over the inner plateau where once-mighty mountains of a million or more years ago have been weathered into elusive, amorphous shapes whose highest places – and some are still six thousand feet high – are no longer shaggy peaks but have become gently rounded domes. In most parts of the North the ice sheet scraped away the soils and sediments accumulated through the millennia, but on the plateaus of the Western Highland the silts and sediments lie so thick that one can fly over them for many hundreds of miles and see no rock outcrops even on the highest hills.

Because they were never denuded of their soils, the plateaus are remarkably fertile. Between two hundred and fifty thousand and five hundred thousand acres of arable land exist in Yukon Territory, although only a few thousand have so far been put to agricultural use. Forests of commercial timber extend much farther north here than anywhere else in Canada. Apart from alpine tundra high on mountain slopes, and the wet tundra of the Porcupine Plains far to the north, tree life in one form or another occupies most of the Western Highland. Animal life is, or was, spectacularly abundant and varied. Along with caribou and moose, the Western Highland still harbours many animals found nowhere else in the Canadian North: Dall sheep, mountain goats, cougars and tiny, rabbit-like pikas are some of these. Grizzly, black and brown bears can be embarrassingly abundant. Great runs of salmon come thousands of miles from the Pacific up the central artery of the Yukon River and into most of its main tributaries.

Although the Western Highland owes its wealth of fauna and flora to its escape from the ice, that escape left man a legacy he has valued even more – rich deposits of placer gold.

Placer gold accumulates as erosion gradually eats away the parent rock and the gold-bearing quartz is ground down in the natural rolling-mills of streams and rivers. In pieces ranging in size from microscopic flecks to fist-sized nuggets the heavy free gold sinks to the stream bottoms. It was the presence of this placer gold in the Yukon River and its tributaries that brought about one of the major paradoxes in the story of the Canadian North.

At the end of the nineteenth century the Yukon region suddenly filled the world's eye to become better known internationally than all the rest of Canada put together. Its freakish rise to prominence began in August, 1896, when squaw-man George Carmack and his Indian companions "Skookum" Jim and "Tagish" Charlie found gold in the bed of Bonanza Creek near the present site of Dawson. So began the greatest gold rush in history. English peers, Transylvanian peasants, southern planters, Finnish reindeer herdsmen, Australian diggers, Maori tribesmen – men and women from at least fifty nations – began to hustle like lemmings toward one of the remotest corners of the known world. Nobody can now say how many actually reached their destination, but a figure of eighty thousand is probably not far off the mark.

This massive wave of immigrants into the Western Highland caught Canada off balance. Although the Yukon region had been defined as a "provisional" district of the Northwest Territories in 1895, there was nothing in the area to represent government. During the first months of the great Klondike rush, anarchy prevailed to such an extent that the United States contemplated moving into the vacuum "to protect its own nationals." If she *had* moved in we can be sure she would never have moved out again. But whatever plans she may have had were scotched when Ottawa hurriedly rushed small detachments of the military and the North West Mounted Police into the Western Highland to plant the flag.

Chaos was reduced to a semblance of order and in 1897 the region became a judicial district. But by the next year the population had increased so much that a bewildered Parliament passed the Yukon Territory Act which gave most of the Western Highland the beginnings of government – one that, by 1908, was supposed to have consisted of a fully elected council as a penultimate step toward provincial status. Yukoners dreamed great dreams in those days. Never before or

151

since had so many Southerners been so willing to make the Canadian North their abode.

But by 1905 the golden phenomenon in Yukon Territory was already fading. Although more than one hundred million dollars in gold had by then been taken from the creek bottoms in the Klondike-Dawson region by small operators, those days were done. Big United States interests such as Guggenheim had begun systematically to take over. Placer mining soon became mechanized and the small miners were rapidly squeezed out by the big dredges that implacably ate their way through private claims. Almost as rapidly as it had been populated, the Yukon was depopulated. Dawson City, which had twenty-five thousand people in 1898 (the largest town Canada has *ever* had in the North), began to shrink at an appalling rate, while nearby towns such as Grand Forks, Gold Bottom, Paris, Caribou and Two Below vanished utterly.

By 1910 nothing much remained of the great Yukon boom except indelible memories, a few intractably individualistic prospectors and the thunderous clankings of huge gold dredges methodically stripping the creek bottoms for the benefit of foreign financiers.

The Klondike gold rush offered us our first real chance to settle the North and to make it a part of the nation. We rejected that opportunity as we have lost every similar opportunity since those days. Need we have done so? Although the big companies have worked and reworked most of the placer gravel several times over and have now abandoned the creeks (the last big dredge ceased working in 1966), a few individuals are still placer mining isolated pockets the dredges could not reach. Not long ago I visited one of these independent operations owned by a man and his wife. In one year this claim yielded more than thirty thousand dollars' worth of gold, making a comfortable living for its owners.

Small-scale placer mining is one of the very few types of mining that does not require huge amounts of capital and equipment. Individuals can make a continuing living at it.

The quarter of a billion dollars in gold taken out of the placer deposits – and out of the country – by the dredging operations of the big companies could have provided a sustaining livelihood for many people in the Klondike region for generations. A mining expert in Dawson City (a forty-year resident) estimated that if the Klondike creeks had remained small holdings (taking into account more effective methods of placer mining developed through the years) they would still be providing a good income for as many as five thousand resident miners and their families. At the time he told me this, Dawson had a population of about six hundred and was little more than a ghost town.

The country for hundreds of miles around Dawson also has a graveyard look. I flew over it in a light aircraft and was appalled by the destruction that had been wrought by the big gold dredges. Well over a thousand miles of the most beautiful and fertile stream and river valleys in the entire North, once vibrantly rich in plants and animals, had been reduced to lifeless slag heaps. Mighty hydraulic hoses had washed the banks of the protecting hills almost down to bedrock, depositing millions of tons of sterile gravel and sand in the valley bottoms. Then the dredges had passed this detritus through their mechanical guts, leaving behind them a wasteland of gigantic worm casts which will support no living thing for countless years to come. What the glaciers failed to do to the myriad living valleys of the upper Yukon River system, man succeeded in doing all too well. It is not a view tourists see. That is perhaps as well, for it is a vision of desolation and destruction fit to convince one that, verily, mankind is mad.

It seems astonishing that Canada and Canadians learned nothing from the sad saga of the Klondike, yet it must be so for across the whole length and breadth of Canada North the same bleak tale of wholesale wastage and rapine is still being acted out.

The Yukon is at present little more than a romantic name

153

to most southern Canadians but if we are not much interested in our remote northwestern territory, others are. Early in World War II the U.S.A. decided it needed an overland link to Alaska and so it built the Alcan Highway which enters Yukon Territory from British Columbia near Watson Lake and traverses the southern part of the territory for 800 miles en route to Alaska. Construction of the highway opened south-central Yukon to base metal mining and by 1976 several foreign-based companies were exporting zinc, lead, silver, copper and asbestos to the value of two hundred million dollars annually. Of this amount Canada received a mere *five* million in taxes, duties and royalties, but the nation had to spend that much and *more* to provide and maintain transportation, social and other facilities for the mines and the company towns. The mines employ about a thousand people, but the majority are newcomers to the territory who will have little choice but to leave when the mines have been depleted, as the Klondikers left so many years ago.

Governed through a Commissioner appointed by the Minister of Indian Affairs and Northern Development in Ottawa, denied either encouragement or opportunity to develop secondary industries based on its mineral wealth, and deprived of all but a pauper's portion of the profits accruing from current exploitation, Yukon Territory is, as it has remained since Klondike times: a classic example of exploitative colonialism in action.

But mineral exploitation is not the whole of the Yukon's sorry story. As elsewhere in the North, oil and gas have become the basis for a new boom. On the broad Porcupine Plains in the north of the territory seismic surveys criss-cross the tundra in such profusion and proximity to one another that an airborne observer has the weird illusion of looking down on endless road allowances laid out to serve some titanic subdivision that is never to be built. These lines were mostly formed by tracked vehicles crushing through the fragile living layer of tundra and exposing the dead, permanently frozen soils beneath. However, once exposed, the underlying matter does not remain frozen. Each passing year sees these wounds thaw deeper and deeper until they form great swampy ditches. These are to be found right across the Canadian tundra wherever exploration vehicles have passed. Many will never heal but will grow deeper and wider with the years. They are among the many permanent scars left by a new nemesis in the North.

The great steel snakes – the gas and oil pipelines – are coming too. Already a gas line from British Columbia has thrust a few score miles into the southeastern corner of Yukon Territory to tap a small gas field in that region. And in May, 1976, Northwest Pipeline Corporation, of Salt Lake City, Utah, announced it was applying for permission to build a major gas pipeline across the Yukon from the Prudhoe Bay fields on the north Alaskan coast, to connect with the British Columbia and Alberta systems, in order to transport gas from Prudhoe to the main body of the United States. A competitive proposal, made several years ago, and much favoured by the federal government of Canada, is for an even larger pipeline from Prudhoe Bay which will cut eastward across the top of Yukon Territory on its way to the lower Mackenzie River valley, there to be joined by lines from the Mackenzie Delta and – it is hoped – from as-yet-untapped offshore fields before turning south through the upper valley of the Mackenzie on its way to Alberta, and thence to the United States.

The two hundred Loucheux Indians of Old Crow, which is on the banks of the Porcupine River and is at once the most northerly and one of the last native settlements in Yukon Territory to retain some semblance of self-sufficiency, view this new threat to their ancient hunting grounds with chill foreboding. They have reason. Yukon Territory differs from most of the remainder of the North in that its white population has for long outnumbered the surviving native peoples with the result that what is now being attempted by white Southerners in Nouveau Quebec, Labrador and the Northwest Territories has very nearly become a *fait accompli*

155

in the Yukon where Indians and Métis alike have been consistently and ruthlessly swept aside by that unholy trinity: Progress, Development and Profit. Nor had they, in the past, any effective means of defending themselves or their rights, for no Indian or Métis sat on the Yukon Territorial Council or held a position of any rank in the territorial government. As for the Department of Indian Affairs and Northern Development whose nominal wards they were – and to whom they might reasonably have looked for protection of their interests – the Department was, and is, in effect, the government of Yukon Territory and has always favoured white interests before those of the native peoples. Because they had never entered into a treaty with the Crown and therefore did not even have the dubious protection of treaty rights, the Indians had found themselves forced to exist as best they might on the contemptuous and niggardly charity of the alien society which had dispossessed them and which was becoming increasingly intolerant of the people whose world it had usurped.

Yet by a strange turn of fate the failure of the federal government to conclude a treaty with the Yukon Indians has suddenly begun to work to the Indians' advantage. Prior to 1973 the federal government had firmly refused to recognize that any such thing as aboriginal rights even existed in Canada. However, in August of that year – in part because of pressure from the newly formed Indian and Eskimo association and their southern white supporters, but mainly as the result of a precedent-making court decision in Yellowknife which implied legal recognition of aboriginal rights – the cabinet reversed its long-standing policy and decided it had better negotiate settlements of land claims in those regions under federal jurisdiction where no treaties had been concluded with the original inhabitants.

Negotiations with the Yukon native peoples were duly begun late in 1973; but the Indians and Métis proved far less malleable than had been anticipated and little progress was made until, at the end of 1975, the government sent in a new negotiator, Digby Hunt, an assistant deputy minister in the Department of Indian Affairs and Northern Development, a director of Panarctic Oils Limited, and a man whom many people believe to be one of the most powerful partisans of the Department's policy of opening up the North to massive resource exploitation. Working in an atmosphere of total secrecy, Hunt and his team of lawyers and other experts soon hammered out a draft agreement with the four inexperienced Indian and Métis negotiators. Hunt then took the draft to Ottawa where, in early May, it was given cabinet approval.

In essence the agreement would have granted the native peoples title to a mere 1,200 square miles – about half of one percent – of Yukon Territory's 207,000 square miles. The native peoples would also have held some rights to (mainly for hunting and fishing), but *not* ownership of, an additional 17,000 square miles, together with permission to *buy* another 200 square miles from the Crown at current market value! There was also to have been a money settlement of $20 million when the agreement was ratified, together with an additional $15 million to be paid over a period of five years thereafter. Although at first glance this seemed like an overwhelming sum to the Indian negotiators, it in fact meant a payment of a little less than $7,000.00 for each individual native person in the Yukon. However, to sweeten the offer the Indians and Métis were promised 25 percent of any royalties the Crown might in future collect from mining activities on as-yet-unexploited Crown lands. They were told this might amount to as much as an additional $45 million. In exchange, all that the native peoples were required to do was to agree that their hereditary claims to, and rights in, the vast remainder of the lands which had once been theirs would be extinguished forever.

Hunt had apparently fulfilled his superior's expectations of him and Ottawa was delighted with the results. But not for long. When Hunt returned to Whitehorse late in May to supervise the ratification of the agreement, he found that the native negotiators with whom he had dealt had been dismissed by the General Assembly of Yukon Indians. Furthermore, the amiable leader of the Indian team, 67-year-old Chief Elijah Smith, had been deposed as President of the Council for Yukon Indians and replaced by a tough-minded 26-year-old, Daniel Johnson, chief of the Kluane Tribal Brotherhood. As for the negotiations ... well, the Council blandly informed Hunt these would have to be postponed for "an indefinite period of time."

Subsequently, the members of the Council for Yukon Indians were not being very forthcoming about their plans, and perhaps wisely so. Nevertheless, one of the native people, who does not wish to be identified, had this to say:

> "The whole story of white people's deals with Indian people has always been full of tricks and bribery and pressure tactics. Look at the old treaties! Look at what happened to the Cree people and the Inuit people of Quebec just a year or two ago! Well, it isn't going to happen in the Yukon .... White people can't bribe us or trick us into giving away our lands anymore .... Sure, we'll negotiate some more, but next time they better keep their tricksters home in Ottawa where they belong ... [and] when they talk to us again they better do it out in the open where all our people can know what's going on .... They better start to listen to the people like they are *people* too – not like they are a bunch of shiftless bums with no brains who they can buy and sell to suit themselves."

IX

The Great River

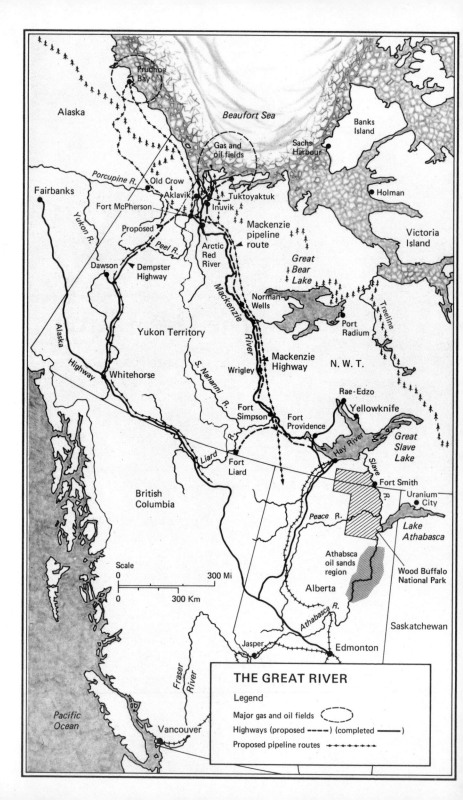

THE GREAT RIVER

Legend

Major gas and oil fields

Highways (proposed - - - -) (completed ——)

Proposed pipeline routes ·+·+·+·+·+·

The two longest rivers in North America both have their headwaters in western Alberta. The most northerly waters of the one become the Milk River and flow southeast into the Missouri, then into the Mississippi and so to the Gulf of Mexico. The most southerly waters of the other rise in the Columbia Ice Field near Jasper, becoming the Athabasca River which later becomes the Slave (joined by the Peace) and finally becomes the Mackenzie, which flows into the Arctic Ocean at the Beaufort Sea. The mouths of these two rivers are thirty-two hundred miles apart in a direct line, yet their headwaters lie within three hundred miles of each other. One is the Great River of the South, the other is the Great River of the North.

The Great River of the North is a good deal more than the stretch that bears Mackenzie's name. The Mackenzie River is only the mighty final flume for a network of many rivers, including the Clearwater, Athabasca, Finlay, Peace, Hay, Liard and Peel, together with scores of lesser streams. Among them they drain northward to the polar ocean a basin of seven hundred thousand square miles that includes one-third of Yukon Territory, better than a quarter of British Columbia, more than half of Alberta, one-third of Saskatchewan and most of the District of Mackenzie.

Fierce, foaming rivers from the mountains to the west; placid, muddy rivers from the poplar plains to the south; clear, green waters from the coniferous forests to the east; and brown-stained waters from the tundra to the northeast

161

all draw together to flow through a gargantuan trough extending northward from the Central Plain of North America, which is itself the bed of an ancient, shallow ocean that once split North America in two. The trough's underlying rocks are sedimentary, favourable to the discovery of oil and natural gas – products of the decay of astronomically large numbers of animals and plants – and finds of both gas and oil have been located from Texas north to the mouth of the Mackenzie.

The valley of the Great River of the North has been more recently shaped to its present watery purpose by a prong of the great ice sheet which thrust westward some ten thousand years ago until it encountered the Mackenzie Mountains. Unable to surmount them, the ice turned north to plow a deep channel hundreds of miles wide to the Arctic coast. As it moved west, the ice gouged a necklace of mighty lakes around the rim of the Canadian Shield. Three of the largest, which now help to feed the Great River, are Lake Athabasca, Great Slave and Great Bear lakes. Great Bear and Great Slave both have an area of roughly twelve thousand square miles, which makes each of them a third again as large as Lake Ontario.

Like its sister to the south the main artery of the Great River of the North is a placid, broad and easy-flowing monster; but unlike its southern sister, it flows through few pastoral scenes. Its way lies mostly through a forested valley where spruce and birch crowd to the river banks, giving way to open tundra only near the mouth of its huge and complex delta.

In the old days travellers going "down North" on its broad waters began their journeys at the head-of-rail at Athabasca Landing, eighty miles north of Edmonton. From here, by canoe or York boat, and later by small stern- or side-wheel steamers, freight and passengers headed down the Athabasca River toward the Arctic coast, passing by miles of tar sands made black and sticky by crude oil seeping up from the depths. These deposits are now being strip-mined by a number of multi-national oil companies (amongst them Exxon, Gulf and Cities Service) with the blessings of, and lavish financial assistance from, the governments of Canada, Alberta and Ontario to the tune of more than a billion dollars – in addition to which the exploiting companies are to receive *two billion* dollars in tax remissions on future sales. Economists have called this, with good reason, the greatest subsidized give-away of natural resources in Canadian history.

Scientists of many disciplines (including some in the employ of government and industry) are deeply perturbed by the forthcoming mammoth disruption of hundreds of square miles of virgin taiga forests as the oil sands are strip-mined. But they are even more apprehensive about what will happen when the first Syncrude Company plant begins operations in 1978 with a daily emission of about three hundred tons of highly poisonous sulphur dioxide gas from its stacks. When the additional plants which are already planned are added to the complex, the emission rate will rise to more than a thousand tons a day; and unless a way, and a will, can be found to prevent it, this outpouring of noxious gas will kill forests and poison lakes and rivers over additional thousands of square miles.

The likelihood of effective pollution controls being imposed by the Alberta government seems small indeed in view of the fact that the one plant already in operation – the Great Canadian Oil Sands refinery – has been allowed to consistently exceed generous government limits on sulphur dioxide discharge ever since it began operations in 1967. Furthermore, for at least four years both the Alberta Department of the Environment and Environment Canada (the federal body charged with pollution control) have been aware that the Great Canadian Oil Sands plant has been illegally discharging up to 400,000 gallons a day of "acutely toxic" waste water into the Athabasca River; yet *neither* agency has taken any action to force the company to halt this massive pollution of the Great River. Perhaps these agencies, or the governments they served, were deterred by statements made by spokesmen for the industry in May, 1976, to the effect that if environmental controls are tightened, the entire oil sands operation will become "uneconomic" and the oil companies will have to consider terminating them.

Already the Athabasca tar sands story seems well on its way to becoming another classic example of how the real long-term interests of Canada have been–and are being– betrayed.

One hundred miles north of the more recent railhead of Waterways, the river enters the western end of Lake Athabasca close to the old trading post of Fort Chipewyan. Although the settlement is in the doldrums now, for nearly two hundred years it was one of the most important fur posts in the North, frequented both by the woodland Cree Indians and by the Chipewyan Dene.

A hundred miles to the eastward, along the north shore of the lake and in northern Saskatchewan, lies another sort of settlement, Uranium City, which grew up after World War II over some of the richest uranium mines in the world. These mines still poke their headframes into the pale sky, although many were closed in 1967 because of over-production and high operating costs. The little town shows the nervous tension that bespeaks the uncertainty of life in any northern Canadian mining town. How long will it live? When will it die? The demand for more bombs or for more nuclear-powered generating plants will tell the story. Meantime the settlement has discovered that most of its private houses and public buildings alike contain dangerous levels of radon gas. The inhabitants are putting up a brave front, but there is much repressed fear of what the cancer-and-mutation-producing radon gas emanations may have done to them . . . and may still do. Still, radiation poisoning is only one more addition to the long list of hazards to which Canadian miners have long been exposed: arsenic poisoning in gold mines; lead poisoning in zinc mines; lung ailments in asbestos mines. But although mining is not a healthy occupation anywhere in Canada, it is particularly unhealthy in the North where control standards have always been notably lax. It is perhaps not to be wondered at that the native peoples are not greatly charmed by the government's attempts to turn them into miners.

A dozen miles after it leaves the Lake, the Athabasca River is joined by its bigger sister, the Peace, which comes swinging in from northern British Columbia through a valley containing the North's best arable lands. However, a big hydro-electric dam built on the upper Peace in the 1960s by the British Columbia government of W. A. C. Bennett has already caused great and probably irreparable damage to the spreading delta of the Peace, once famed for its extraordinary productivity of ducks, geese and muskrat. Now the Alberta government is proposing to build a series of hydro-electric dams on the lower river, thereby threatening the future of much of the rest of the valley.

The Peace and Athabasca rivers unite to form the Slave River which flows on "down North" across the Alberta border into the Northwest Territories near Forth Smith. This one-time trading post is now the education capital of the Territories. Millions of dollars have been spent here on school facilities designed to impose Ottawa's solution to the problem of what is to be done with the native peoples of the North. The solution is predicated on the theory that assimilation and integration will instill the same witless hunger for material wealth in the native peoples which characterizes the society of southern Canada, and thereby coerce the Indians, Eskimos and Métis into submitting to, if not actually endorsing, the rape of their lands.

However, it begins to look as if this solution will be rejected by the native peoples, partly because of their increasing awareness that the dominant white society has no real intention of ever granting them the equality which they were told would flow from integration.

Not long ago I talked to a young woman of the Slavey Dene who had spent two years in Fort Smith studying to be a teacher. When she went back to her own people it was not as an apostle of government policy but as a fiercely determined opponent.

"You know, right near Fort Smith is a big rapid they call Rapid of the Drowned. In the old days many canoes, and big boats too, got smashed up there and lots of people drowned. Most of them were Dene working for the fur traders. After I spent all that time in Fort Smith, one day I understood – now they are trying to drown *all* the Dene another way. Then I knew I had to go back to my people and fight against what white people were trying to do to us."

The Slave flows on down north, passing lethargically through the reserve of rolling parkland and open prairie which is Wood Buffalo National Park. Here the last large herds of buffalo still survive in a wild state. Outside the park, small free-ranging herds become targets for wealthy southern hunters whose egos need the satisfaction to be found in killing beasts bigger than themselves.

Two hundred miles north of Lake Athabasca the short-lived Slave River ends in Great Slave Lake, along whose northwestern and southwestern shores cluster more than half the white residents of the entire Northwest Territories. On the south side of the lake is the town of Hay River, the major transportation centre for the valley of the Mackenzie. To it, by rail and road, comes freight from the South destined for points as far away as Prudhoe Bay on the north coast of Alaska, and Spence Bay in the eastern Arctic. At Hay River much of this freight is trans-shipped into fleets of barges propelled by diesel tugs, to begin the long trip down the Mackenzie to the Arctic Ocean.

Hay River is a white man's town full of entrepreneurs

who see the future in terms of steadily expanding "northern development." The native residents, mostly Métis and Slavey Dene, have been relegated to the position of second-class citizens and have little or no share in Hay River's prosperity.

Pine Point, some forty miles to the east of Hay River, was one of the largest mining developments in Canada when it began operations in 1966. Its lead-zinc deposits annually produce four million tons of ore whose concentrates, valued at 180 million dollars in 1975, are shipped south on a 437-mile railroad especially built by the Canadian government for this purpose. Pine Point epitomizes the Canadian attitude toward the North. No smelter has been built to give jobs to local residents. Instead most of the concentrate is shipped all the way to a refinery at Trail, B.C. This is in direct opposition to the belief of many economists that raw resources should be processed as fully as possible in the area where they are found, both because this makes sound economic sense and because it gives rise to permanent settlements, rather than to the temporary boom-and-bust kind which continues to characterize northern Canada.

On the north shore of the lake, opposite Pine Point, is another town that began life as a mining community – Yellowknife – whose stock in trade through several decades was gold. By the mid-1960s the high-grade ore had been largely exhausted and the big companies, Consolidated Mining and Smelting, and Giant, were preparing to close down. Yellowknife would have become at least a temporary ghost town had not the federal government decided to make it the capital of the Northwest Territories. The mines have continued in operation because of the phenomenal (though perhaps short-lived) rise in gold prices but, as is increasingly the case in so many northern communities, it is the presence of the multi-faceted paraphernalia of government which now gives

167

the place its major *raison d'être*. In 1976 government personnel and their dependents in the Northwest Territories numbered nearly 12,000, of whom the largest proportion lived in Yellowknife.

Hay River, Pine Point and Yellowknife are touted as being bright symbols of northern progress, but there are other communities in the Great Slave area as well. There is, for instance, the twin community of Rae-Edzo some sixty airmiles northwest of Yellowknife. Here live most of the surviving Dogrib Dene, some in the old hamlet of Fort Rae and some in a new community known as Edzo, fifteen miles distant. The nearly 1,300 Dogribs concentrated in this one small region cannot support themselves upon the dwindling animal resources in the surrounding area and so are forced to rely more and more on welfare. The Department of Indian Affairs has made considerable efforts to turn them into northern mine workers, a job that very few other Canadians find appealing. In fact the mines at Yellowknife are having to import immigrant Italians to work underground, and the Dene are content to let them.

"Lots of money to make in the mines," a young Dogrib told me, "if that's what you want. What *we* want is to live *on* the land like always, not down in a hole. Money is not so much. We think it is the *way* you live that counts."

Yellowknife and Hay River between them guard the gates to the Mackenzie Valley and dominate the lives of all who live to the northward along the banks of the Great River and its tributaries. It is a dominance which began with the arrival of the first traders in the latter part of the eighteenth century and which has been exercised ever since by a minority of white intruders over a majority of native inhabitants. It is a dominance which, through the better part of two centuries, has been racist, exploitive and oppressive – and it remains so to this day.

Now, however, it is being challenged. As a government official, who for the sake of his job must remain unidentified, told me in the autumn of 1975:

"Remember the old movie cliché with the Great White Hunter and the beautiful blonde sitting by a campfire on the African veldt listening to the sound of drums in the distance? And he says to her: 'Hmmmm, the natives are getting restless,' and reaches for his gun? Don't laugh. The drums are sounding in the North today and don't you believe the Whites can't hear them. If they go for their guns – and there are plenty of rednecks who are talking about doing that – there'll be ructions like this country hasn't seen since Louis Riel's time. Believe me, the palmy colonial days in the North are coming to an end."

Since the early 1970s hostility between the immigrant Whites from the South and the native Cree, Dene and Métis of the Great River country has been rapidly mounting. The immediate cause is that the major thrust of the massed battalions of industry and government, in their joint campaign to "conquer" the North, is being directed down the valley of the Mackenzie. The native peoples of the valley clearly perceive this as a final fatal thrust destined to end their way of life, deprive them of their lands, and fling them aside like so much flotsam cast up by a tidal wave. They know that if they are ever to take a stand in their own defence, they must do so now. Consequently they have renounced the treaties which were imposed upon their people by guile and subterfuge in the early part of this century, on the grounds that not only were these never honoured by the government but that the native peoples were defrauded of something they never intended to part with – their rights to continued possession of their ancestral lands. The Dene and the Métis, who are the most affected, began by adopting a calm and reasonable approach in attempting to negotiate with their colonial overlords for a new deal. They made it clear that they were not arbitrarily opposed to development – as distinct from exploitation – of their portion of the North, but before any such development began they believed they were entitled to a settlement of their land claims, together with guarantees which would enable them to maintain the way of life they wished to pursue, and which would also ensure for them a share of the returns resulting from the use of their land and its resources. As James Wah-shee, first president of the Northwest Territories Indian Brotherhood, put it: "What we seek is the means to avoid the destruction of the land and of our people, and a democratic right to take our place in the economic, social and political future of the Northwest Territories."

It was only after these requests had been brusquely swept aside by Ottawa that the first faint sound of drumbeats began to be heard.

Smouldering resentment against the injustices inflicted on them in the past, combined with the denial by government either of redress for their grievances or recognition of their rights, led to the promulgation in the summer of 1975 of the Dene Declaration which states that the native peoples of the Territories must regain control of their own destinies – peacefully, if possible, but by whatever methods circumstances may dictate.

The reaction of the Canadian government was indicated in a statement made in April, 1976, by Judd Buchanan, Minister of Indian Affairs and Northern Development, at Yellowknife, whither he had gone to make a speech praising "northern development" to a group of businessmen. Buchanan dismissed the Dene Declaration as "gobbledegook that a Grade 10 student could have written in 15 minutes." This from the man who is charged by Parliament to protect the interests of the native peoples of the North.

The stand the Dene feel they have been forced to take is producing near-paranoic anger among the white residents of the Territories, many of whom see the Indian demands as a threat to their acquisition of the easy riches which "northern development" promises. In the days when similar riches were to be garnered from the fur trade, Whites in the North thought of the native peoples as a useful resource. Now, in the opinion of many Whites both in and out of the North, the native peoples have become an encumbrance to progress. As the head of a Calgary-based company which stands to gain lucrative contracts for work in the Mackenzie Valley puts it: "If people can't, or won't, make the best use of their land they don't deserve [to have] it. They have to stand aside and let someone who can really do something take over."

The attitude of the majority of Whites in the valley of the Great River toward the native population is epitomized in a report printed in the Toronto *Globe and Mail* on May 8, 1976:

SPEAKER OF N.W.T. HOUSE TELLS BERGER HE'S UNWANTED AND SHOULD LEAVE NORTH
By Nancy Cooper

YELLOWKNIFE. A prominent Northerner has told Mr. Justice [Thomas] Berger that he is unliked and unwanted in the North and that he should go home.

David Searle, Q.C., Speaker of the House in the Northwest Territories government and former president of the Yellowknife Liberal Association, used the annual meeting of the Northwest Territories Mental Health Association to tee off on the British Columbia Supreme Court judge who for the past 14 months has been conducting an inquiry into the likely effects of building a natural gas pipeline down the Mackenzie Valley.

Mr. Searle who represents the City of Yellowknife on Territorial Council . . . feels the presence of people like Mr. Justice Berger [is] having a bad influence on the North . . . he charged "leftwingers from the South" with "spreading a sluggish sickness among our innocent and idealistic native peoples."

Mr. Searle, who said he was speaking personally, thinks social services have to be drastically cut in the North. He wants family allowances abolished, legal aid reduced, unemployment insurance tightened and stringent environment controls loosened. Fewer schools should be built and he wants to see federal grants to native groups cut off.

In an interview later Mr. Searle simply explained that he was saying publicly what many white northern government, business and professional people have been telling him privately . . . . Mr. Searle, a lawyer, has appeared before Mr. Justice Berger during the pipeline inquiry on behalf of the Chambers of Commerce in the North . . . .

The northern Whites have "gone for their guns" and Searle's outburst was the opening shot in what will doubtless be a well-orchestrated and well-financed campaign to turn any sympathy which southern Canadians may have had for the northern natives into anger and resentment against them for standing in the way of Northern Progress. The campaign will depict the northern people either as childlike incompetents who cannot be trusted to look after themselves, or as welfare bums, chronic alcoholics, whining malcontents, dupes of "left-wing agitators" and, in general, as the sort of people who deserve nothing but contempt.

Although the federal government may take no overt part in this campaign, it will be well content to see it develop. Despite what has been claimed to the contrary by government propagandists, the federal authorities have never been prepared to assist the native peoples with more than peripheral medical and health assistance, submarginal housing and social services, and just enough education to infect them with southern appetites. Canada has had no real choice in giving them this much since the alternative – to allow them to perish outright as they *were* perishing only a few short decades ago – would now be politically unacceptable in the eyes of the rest of the world. Nevertheless, Ottawa seems determined to prevent the native peoples from obtaining and exercising any real control over their own destiny and, more particularly, over what is to be done to, and in, the land which once was theirs alone. In the valley of the Great River this means excluding them from any say in the grandiose plan hatched by Ottawa and its business associates for what is called the Mackenzie Valley Corridor. This is to be a mighty transportation complex running from the shore of the Beaufort Sea to southern Canada and it is slated to include a truck highway, a railroad, multiple oil and gas pipelines, and a high-capacity electricity transmission system. The Corridor is not intended to be a two-way street designed to bring to the North whatever advantages southern Canada possesses; it is solely and singlemindedly designed to siphon the resources of the North southward to the industrial heartlands of the United States and, to a lesser degree, to Canada as well, with maximum efficiency and dispatch.

The Great River of the North takes on Mackenzie's name as it leaves Great Slave Lake, swinging westward until it brings up against the massive wall of the Mackenzie Mountains, then turning north for a two-hundred-mile run between majestic ranges. At the northern end of this run it is joined by the Great Bear River flowing out of the lake of the same name which lies eighty miles to the eastward. Great Bear Lake is a mecca for wealthy sport fishermen, and from any one of several lodges around its shores one can catch lake trout weighing up to fifty pounds, while paying as much as $1,000 a week for the privilege. Almost all of these lodges are owned and patronized by Americans. Commercial fishing by native residents is not allowed: the whole lake is set aside for the use of southern sportsmen.

There are several old fur trade settlements along the Mackenzie River between Great Slave Lake and Great Bear River, and in most of these the native residents are banding together to present a common front against the wave of change. Fort Providence and Fort Simpson are exceptions because the north-thrusting Mackenzie Highway has already overrun them, turning them into tawdry way stations on the "Road to Resources." In both these places the native peoples have been unceremoniously pushed aside, as they have been in Yellowknife and Hay River, to become second- or third-rate citizens living in slum conditions in islands of despair.

The people of Wrigley, Fort Norman and Fort Franklin (which have remained almost purely native settlements) were alerted to their danger by what happened to Forts Providence and Simpson. In 1975 the Slavey Dene of Wrigley showed such determined opposition to the approaching highway that the authorities were forced to halt construction. When work is resumed Wrigley will be by-passed – one small victory for the people of the North.

Farther downriver lie Fort McPherson and Arctic Red River, one-time citadels of the fur trade which are still home to the Loucheux Dene. They also hang in the balance of an uncertain future as the Dempster Highway from the Yukon reaches out toward them; but their residents are even more apprehensive about the arrival of a pipeline. Nevertheless, the people in these villages are prepared to make a stand against any new encroachments on their lives. Philip Blake, a 34-year-old Loucheux from Fort McPherson, described how his people felt, in testimony given before the inquiry being conducted by Judge Thomas Berger.

"Mr. Berger, I am not an old man but I have seen many changes in my life. Fifteen years ago most of what you see today in Fort McPherson did not exist. Take a look around the community now and you will get an idea of what has happened to the Indian people here over the past few years.

"Mr. Berger, do you think this is the way the Indian people would have chosen to live if we had any choice? Do you think we would have divided the community [into a modern White town and an Indian ghetto] and given ourselves worse housing than the transient Whites? Take a look at the school here. Try to find something, anything, that makes it a place where Indian values and traditions are respected. Can you really believe we have chosen to have high rates of suicide and social breakdown? Do you think we would have chosen to become beggars in our own homeland?

"We have never tried to conquer new frontiers, or outdo our parents, or make sure that every year we are richer than before. We have been satisfied to see our wealth as *ourselves and our land*. It is our greatest wish to pass this land on to our grandchildren in the same condition we got it from our fathers.

"But, Judge Berger, if your nation chooses to continue to try to destroy our nation, then I hope you will understand that we are willing to fight so our nation can survive. It is *our* world and we are willing to defend it for ourselves, our children and their children. If your nation becomes so violent it would tear up our country, destroy our society and occupy our homeland, then of course we will have no choice but to react with violence.

"I hope we do not have to do this, for it is not the way we would choose. However, if we are forced to blow up the pipeline, I hope you will not look only at the violence of the Indian action but also on the violence of your own nation which would force us to take such a course."

Since March of 1975, at hearings in every community in the whole of the northwestern region which will be affected by gas and oil exploration, production, and pipelines, Mr. Justice Thomas Berger has listened patiently and with understanding to hundreds of people like Blake. Because of these hearings the voices of the native peoples are at last being heard, if faintly, in the distant South. The federal government, which one suspects set up the inquiry in the first place only as a publicity device to demonstrate its apparent interest in the wellbeing of the native peoples, has not been pleased with Berger's work. Attempts were made to halt or limit the inquiry; but these met with such resistance from native organizations, sympathetic members of the press, and white supporters in the South, that they came to nothing. If the northern people ever do succeed in obtaining justice at southern hands, it will be in large part due to the work of Judge Tom Berger. If they do *not*, it will be thanks to the supporters of the oil and gas industry both in and out of government – men such as Mr. Rod Sykes, Mayor of Calgary, which is the so-called oil capital of Canada.

At a hearing held in Calgary before Judge Berger himself on May 13, 1976, Mayor Sykes stigmatized the inquiry as "a disastrous and costly mistake."

> "I am amazed that Canadians have tolerated so far and even financed the talk about land claims and compensation claims by people who would in many cases rather talk than work .... I believe we have had enough of the politics of blackmail and intimidation ... and we expect government to deal decisively with this intolerable situation ... [the inquiry] has provided a platform for troublemakers, domestic and imported, threatening the energy resource supplies of all Canadians .... In the name of freedom of speech and the right to be heard, people whose fundamental interest is self-interest rather than the national interest have exploited the process."

Below Arctic Red River the Great River scents the sea and splays out into the Mackenzie Delta. This is a fabulous world: more than fifteen hundred square miles of intricately braided channels, innumerable ponds, sloughs and muskeg swamps – the whole alive with waterfowl and muskrats. Not so long ago it was one of the most productive trapping areas in the world. In 1950 Indian and Eskimo trappers took 300,-000 muskrat pelts from it and sold them for an average of two dollars each. Aklavik, in the middle of the Delta, was

176

then the muskrat capital of the North and its mostly native residents were as prosperous as they had any desire to be.

However, in 1954 the federal government began building a new town to the east of the Delta. Ostentatiously named Inuvik, which means Place of the People, it was designed to be the showplace of the New North. At a cost of many millions of dollars a complex of residential schools (in duplicate, for Protestants and Catholics), hospitals, administrative buildings, hotels, apartments and elegant modern homes was erected around a multi-branched umbilicus called a Utilidor, which was designed to solve the problems of servicing a town built on permafrost. This self-heating, boxlike structure brought running water and steam heat to, and carried sewage away from, those buildings which were to be occupied by government officials, nurses, teachers, scientists, sociologists, police, preachers, and other Whites from the South who were deemed indispensable to the success of the community.

Meanwhile the Indians, Eskimos and Métis of Aklavik had been told that they must abandon their town and move to the fine new "city" of Inuvik, despite the fact that Inuvik was almost impossibly distant from the muskrat trapping grounds upon which their livelihood depended. Once arrived in the model city of the North they found they were expected to live in Inuvik West, which lay outside the "Utilidor Palace." Since the area reserved for them had no running water and no sewage system, as well as far too few of the tiny, jerry-built houses which were considered adequate for natives, Inuvik West soon became Canada's newest slum. To complicate matters the new residents, for whom Inuvik had supposedly been built, discovered that the small amount of employment their new town offered was mostly as janitors, servants and maintenance men for the Whites in Inuvik East.

After a short time many of the ungrateful natives began to leave. They made their way back to Aklavik where they dug in their heels until, eventually, a reluctant government was forced to accept the inevitable and permit Aklavik to endure. It is now one of the more viable settlements in the region and a centre of resistance against the proponents of instant change and untrammelled "development." It may be noted that in the Eskimo language *aklavik* means Place of the Barren-Ground Grizzly Bear, a powerful but peaceful beast . . . unless and until he is roused to act in his own defence.

Inuvik has meanwhile become the jumping-off point for scores of southern companies, most of them foreign owned, hotly engaged in a race to secure resource claims throughout the whole of the western Canadian Arctic. It is also a service depot for oil and gas exploration in the Mackenzie Delta region and offshore in the Beaufort Sea, and it is the administrative centre for the area. Its problems of alcoholism, prostitution, violent crime and social breakdown are massive, owing in large part to the passage through it of great numbers of transients participating in the northern boom. One Eskimo, who lived in Inuvik until he could stand it no longer, recently summed up the native peoples' feelings toward the place:

> "If Inuvik is an example of what government and business between them are going to do for us and our country, we'd better get clear of them while there's still time; or maybe put a wall up around Inuvik, because it sure as hell is a plague spot."

Inuvik, together with the settlement of Tuktoyaktuk out on the northeastern corner of the Delta, is experiencing the full impact of the boom as more and more wells are drilled in the vicinity. Several exploratory holes sunk in the late 1960s demonstrated the presence of oil and gas; but it soon became clear that these and many later wells (about one hundred had been sunk by 1976), which had been drilled on or not far inland from the coast, were probing the southern periphery of what promised to be a truly immense field (perhaps as large as, or larger than, the fabulous field at Prudhoe Bay), the bulk of which lay under the waters of the Beaufort Sea.

The international oil companies (which own almost all the leases both on shore and off the coast) became very anxious to begin offshore drilling – but there was a problem.

In 1971 the Canadian government banned drilling in the Georgia Strait on the Pacific coast because the risk of blow-outs (even in those protected and ice-free southern waters) and the consequent likelihood of major damage being inflicted on the coasts of British Columbia were unacceptable to the people of that province. This decision established a precedent which Ottawa could not readily ignore by allowing the oil companies to openly undertake drilling in the Beaufort Sea where the risks were infinitely greater. Obviously, if the welfare of the people of British Columbia was of paramount importance, the same principle should have held true for the native peoples of the Canadian Arctic coast.

It should have – but it did not. Working in close co-operation with the oil companies, the Department of Indian Affairs and Northern Development set itself to find a way of circumventing the Georgia Strait precedent. It proceeded under a shroud of secrecy. All important documents relating to the subject were stamped "Restricted" or "Confidential" and only senior officials of the oil companies, of the Department of Indian Affairs and Northern Development, the National Energy Board and, presumably, some members of the federal cabinet, knew what was afoot.

The solution was a masterpiece of subterfuge. The oil companies (mainly Imperial Oil, which is a subsidiary of Exxon, and Sun Oil) were allowed to begin drilling from *artificial* islands constructed of gravel, mud and concrete. These operations were then publicly identified and were actually licensed as *normal land-use* explorations instead of as the offshore drilling operations which they really were. The first drill hole from an artificial island was completed by Imperial in 1973. A total of eight have now been drilled and several have struck gas or oil, while at least one – fortunately a dry one – has since been destroyed by storms and winter ice.

Another and related marvel of chicanery was also concocted during the 1970s. The story of this one is involved but singularly instructive.

Soon after the discovery in 1968 of the immense oil and gas fields at Prudhoe Bay in northern Alaska, the oil companies began to bring great pressure on the Canadian government to throw wide the doors to Canadian gas and oil exports to the U.S.A. The oil industry claimed this action was necessary because Canadian reserves of hydrocarbons were enormously in excess of any foreseeable Canadian needs. The then-Minister of Energy, Joe Greene, himself announced that in 1970 Canada's oil reserves amounted to 469 billion barrels while natural gas reserves stood at 725 trillion cubic feet. At 1970 rates of consumption, he told Canadians, these reserves represented 923 years' supply of oil and 329 years' supply of gas.

Although the figures Greene quoted were official in the sense that they had come to him through federal energy agencies, they were actually derived – as he must have known – from the oil and gas industry itself. There was no government or independent assessment of their accuracy; and yet, unbelievable as it must seem, the federal cabinet accepted them as being totally reliable when, as subsequent events proved and as any reasonably intelligent person ought to have suspected at the time, they had been exaggerated on a monumental scale. It is hardly to be doubted that they were deliberately inflated in order to panic Canadians into accepting the oil industry's contention that it should be permitted to export as much southern Canadian gas and oil as quickly as possible before supplies from Prudhoe Bay could begin to arrive on U.S. markets and so leave Canada in the dire situation of having no purchaser for her super-abundant "surplus."

Speaking before the National Energy Board in the middle of 1970 on the urgent necessity of increasing hydrocarbon exports to the U.S.A., Jean-Luc Pépin, Minister of Industry, Trade and Commerce, had this to say:

"It would be crazy to sit on it [Canada's reputedly gigantic oil and gas reserves]. In maybe twenty-five or fifty years we'll be heating ourselves from the rays of the sun and then we'll kick ourselves for not capitalizing on what we had when gas and oil was a current commodity."

Mr. Pépin's apparent ignorance of the realities of the situation is astounding. Even assuming that he and his cabinet colleagues had been gullible enough to swallow the oil companies' estimates, how could he not have been aware that the greatest value to be derived from natural gas and oil is not in their use as simple fuels but as basic raw materials for the petrochemical industry? How could he have been unaware that there will be an expanding market for gas and oil in this industry as long as modern man has any need of a vast array of products ranging from plastics through medicinal supplies to fertilizers, all of which are produced in great variety and quantity from petrochemicals?

Nevertheless, government ignorance, if that is all it was, served the oil industry's purpose marvellously well. As one example, on September 29, 1970, Energy Minister Greene triumphantly announced that the Trudeau government had approved the largest natural gas export permit in Canadian history – for 6.3 trillion cubic feet to be exported to the U.S.A. over a fifteen- or twenty-year period!

It must always be remembered, and can never be too strongly stressed, that it is not *Canada* but the multi-national oil companies who *own* Canadian gas and oil, and who take the profits from their sale. It is they, not *Canada*, who during 1976 sold over half a million barrels of Canadian oil and three billion cubic feet of natural gas to the U.S.A. *every single day of the year*. These companies are also the real owners of the gas and oil which will come from Prudhoe Bay, the Mackenzie Delta and from under the Beaufort Sea. What they actually set out to do in 1970 was to unload most of the low-cost, easily accessible supplies of southern Canadian gas and oil, in order to establish a seller's market for future sales of their high-cost and even higher-priced oil and gas from the Prudhoe Bay, Mackenzie Delta and Beaufort Sea fields.

Once this had been accomplished there was no further need to maintain the gargantuan fiction that Canada possessed virtually limitless reserves of hydrocarbons. On the contrary, because the oil companies now wanted to engage in extensive drilling off all three oceanic coasts, they wished Canadians to believe the exact opposite – *that the country was threatened with an imminent oil and gas shortage of such proportions that Canada would have to relax even such inadequate environmental controls as then existed.*

By the middle of 1973 Canadians were being told by government and industry alike that the nearly inexhaustible oil and gas reserves of less than three years earlier had mysteriously evaporated. Furthermore – so ran the litany – unless the oil companies were given virtual freedom to do what they thought best in the offshore regions, *and* unless they were permitted to make even larger profits on current sales in order to cover the costs of searching for new supplies, Canada would soon be faced with a catastrophic shortage of hydrocarbons. Canadians were invited to weep for companies like Exxon (which made a *net* profit of 2.5 billion dollars in a single year during this period) that were reporting themselves in dire financial straits as a result of their sacrificial efforts to serve the interests of Canada and Canadians.

Was there and *is* there any immediate danger of a shortage? Since all the basic information on which estimates of reserves are made comes from the oil companies themselves, there is probably no way to be quite sure. Nevertheless, it is the firm opinion of a number of independent experts in the field that the current "shortage" is as highly suspect as the 1970 "surplus" should have been. For example, the Canadian Arctic Resources Committee has calculated that there will be no domestic shortage before 1990, *even if* we continue to allow the oil companies to export our southern supplies of hydrocarbons to the U.S.A. at the present extravagant rate. Furthermore, if Canada were to cancel the export permits granted to the international oil companies, she would have assured supplies of both gas and oil to last nearly to the end of the century, which would allow ample time and opportunity to cautiously explore for, and develop, replacement supplies in the North or elsewhere. This assumes, of course, that Canada would be able to reserve the bulk of any newly found production for her own domestic consumption. This seems a somewhat dubious prospect in the light of what is happening in the Mackenzie Delta.

Although the oil companies drilling in that region claim they have only proved the existence of about seven trillion cubic feet of natural gas, they have already concluded long-term contracts with California gas distributors to supply *them* with *twelve* trillion cubic feet from the Mackenzie Delta fields!

It is true that in May of 1976 the Trudeau cabinet made small, apologetic noises about reclaiming some of this gas for Canada; but considering Ottawa's previous record in protecting Canadian resources for Canadians, not many people are likely to be encouraged to hurry out and buy gas furnaces for their homes.

The truth of the matter is that Canada has proven reserves of energy of every kind sufficient to meet her needs well into the future; but unfortunately most of these are not owned by Canada and therefore are not available to her citizens. In Alberta and British Columbia, for instance, U.S. companies are mining 11 million tons of coal a year and selling it to Japan! Millions upon millions of kilowatts of hydro-generated electricity are being exported to the United States from Ontario and Quebec, and several other provinces. The mere suggestion that this energy, or Canada's supplies of gas and oil, should be retained for Canadian use brings howls of outrage from the captains of industry and

183

their spokesmen in government. Retention would be immoral, they cry, for it would mean that Canada would have to welch on legal contracts. But those contracts are not between *Canada* and the foreign buyers; they are, almost without exception, between individual, mostly foreign-owned industrial corporations and the foreign buyers. If there is immorality, surely it is to be found with those who are permitting Canada to be bled of her energy resources.

Shortly after the first gas and oil was discovered in the Mackenzie Delta, a consortium ironically calling itself Canadian Arctic Gas, the great majority of whose twenty-seven member corporations are foreign owned or controlled (including such giants as Exxon, Shell, Atlantic-Richfield and Standard Oil), applied to the Canadian government for permission to build and operate the world's longest, most expensive and largest gas pipeline, through the Mackenzie Valley southward to the U.S.A. The proposal calls for an initial 48-inch diameter pipe which is later to be twinned. The cost in money for the single line was originally estimated at about six billion dollars, and the current estimate is somewhere around fourteen billion. However, no estimate has ever been offered as to what such a project would cost in terms of social disruption to the residents of the valley, in terms of environmental damage or in terms of financial disruption to the Canadian economy. Furthermore, no provision was made to consult with or to obtain the consent of the people through whose lands the line would pass, and none would have been made by either industry or government if they had had their way.

The Department of Indian Affairs and Northern Development, which was then under the ministerial leadership of Jean Chrétien, gave tacit approval. The National Energy Board of Canada, whose next chairman-to-be was a member of a mixed government-and-industry commission dedicated to the pipeline project, would undoubtedly have rubber-stamped the approval, and the cabinet would have given the required permission had not some unanticipated developments occurred.

One of these was the formation of a public-interest group called the Canadian Arctic Resources Committee, consisting of some of Canada's foremost independent experts in economic, industrial, environmental and northern affairs, including Trevor Lloyd, John Deutsch, Max Dunbar, Douglas Pimlott and Walter Gordon. This group was appalled that such a huge enterprise was about to be undertaken without any real assessment of Canada's need for it; without evaluating its probable effect on the economy – most economists agree that such a massive expenditure will sharply accelerate inflation and increase general interest rates, mortgage rates and the cost of obtaining small-business and personal bank loans – and of its impact on the environment and the peoples of the North.

The Canadian Arctic Resources Committee undertook to unearth, study and publicize the true facts of the matter and bring about disclosure of plans and policies shared by government and industry which had previously been concealed from the public eye. Furthermore, it gave support to the organizations of native peoples in the North who were struggling desperately to make themselves heard in defence of their own lands and way of life. It was certainly in large part due to the efforts of the Canadian Arctic Resources Committee and several similarly concerned groups that the cabinet felt constrained to appoint the Berger inquiry, before giving formal authorization to the Mackenzie Valley pipeline project. That the Berger inquiry would become a thorn in the side of industry and government alike, instead of serving the cosmetic purposes required of most government inquiries and commissions, was something which could hardly have been foreseen.

As a result of "obstructionism" from the public-interest groups, from the political action groups of northern native peoples, and from the Berger inquiry – all of which led to an increasingly sharp and critical appraisal by the news media of the real purposes and objectives of the federal government and the oil and gas industry – the Mackenzie Valley pipeline, originally due to be begun in 1972, had still not been started by the end of 1975. However, Ottawa and the oil interests, together with the U.S. government whose spokesmen have called the pipeline "an American project in the national interest," were determined to brook no further delays. Early in 1976 hearings began before the National Energy Board of Canada to determine which of two competing groups should be allowed to build and operate the line (both national governments clearly favour Canadian Arctic Gas over Foothills Pipelines of Calgary, which is closely associated with a number of U.S. companies and plans to build a smaller, cheaper line).

One of the reasons being publicized by Canadian Arctic Gas to justify the need for an immediate start is the contention that the line is primarily intended to deliver gas from Prudhoe Bay to U.S. midwestern markets which are now beginning to suffer from a gas shortage. However, a much more compelling reason is Canadian Arctic Gas's desire to forestall the attempts of a competing U.S. consortium known as El Paso Alaska Limited which wants to build a line from Prudhoe Bay across Alaska to tidewater on the Pacific Ocean and then ship the gas in liquefied form by supertankers to U.S. West Coast ports. And behind the anxiety of the members of the Canadian Arctic Gas consortium to block the El Paso proposal is their determination to control the exploitation of *all* gas (and oil) resources so far found, and yet to be found, in the Canadian western Arctic, by building, owning and operating a transmission line through the Mackenzie Valley, which would also, of course, carry gas and oil from Prudhoe Bay.

The Canadian Arctic Gas pipeline issue is only a forerunner of what is to come. In 1975 a related consortium, the Beaufort-Delta Oil Project Limited, consisting of three multi-national oil companies and two pipeline companies, announced its intention to file an application to build an oil pipeline from the Delta through the Mackenzie Valley to the U.S.A.

Economist Edgar Dosman spoke nothing more than the simple truth in his book, *The National Interest*, published in 1975, when he concluded:

> "Canada is committed, and has been for some time, to pipelines that will pump our northern oil and gas resources straight to the United States."

The valley of the Great River of the North is taiga country, and the taiga is a world all of its own. Strangers flying over the dark and rippling forests may view it as an alien place, hostile and forbidding. But those who have lived within it, and under its protection, for countless generations have come to value it as the living world it truly is, and have come to love it as the mother of them all.

One day all too soon there may be nothing left to love.

Epilogue
O, Canada! Who stands on guard for thee?

"The task of developing northern Canada is so gigantic that it staggers the imagination. Capital and human resources will be required in such degree as to 'boggle the mind.' It is going to require the combined efforts and resources of all levels of government and the private sectors. I urge that they work together closely so that the North is developed aggressively . . . . I do not agree with those people who would not share our resources with others, particularly our brothers the Americans. Without their help we would still be 'hewers of wood and haulers of water.'"

So writes the editor of *Opportunities in Northern Canada*, a glossy and expensively produced one-shot compendium of hyperbole extolling the rich business opportunities awaiting those who take part in "northern development." It is supported by more than a hundred multi-national and Canadian corporations and by departments of the federal, provincial and territorial governments.

As spokesman and publicist for what he demurely calls "the private sectors" the editor unmistakably heralds the coming-of-age of the newest northern myth with a stirring call to battle. *We are*, he tells us, *committed to a full-scale invasion of the North, and we must use all the weapons at our command in order to ensure success.*

The psychology is the same as that which propagandists have used since time immemorial to whip armies, and even entire nations, into blind, crusading fervour. And like so many similar clarion calls made in the past, this one conceals

189

the attempts of a few to perpetrate a gigantic fraud upon the many.

The naked truth is that those who are urging, seducing and deluding us into mounting a blitzkrieg against the North are motivated by no high purposes, but first and foremost by unadulterated greed – and they are hoping to win *our* allegiance to their cause by appealing to the latent greed in us.

Greed! *Not* need!

The naked truth is that we Canadians are permitting ourselves to be swindled into allowing a massive alienation of our northern resources, not because *Canada* needs those resources now but because foreign buyers can be *found* for them now.

The vision of easy riches, which is a vitally important part of the myth, dazzles our eyes. It is intended to do so. But it is the multi-national cartels, supported by a few self-serving Canadian interests, who will reap the profits. The reward the nation will receive for the betrayal of the North into the hands of alien plunderers will amount to no more than a token payment of Judas' money.

Close to ninety per cent of *all* Canadian northern resources so far discovered are *already owned* directly or indirectly by foreign companies. Most of these resources are already destined to be shipped out of Canada in their raw state to enrich the manufacturing and processing industries of other countries – foremost amongst whom are "our brothers, the Americans, without whose help we would still be 'hewers of wood and haulers of water.'"

It seems self-evident that we cannot look to our present leaders to protect either our interests or those of the unborn generations who will *truly* need the northern resources if they, and Canada, are to survive. The international freebooters of our era command the support of the majority of our elected representatives as well as the support of all too many of the civil servants whose wages we pay. Actively or passively, most of these are collaborating in the betrayal.

190